*To my grandparents:*
*Peter and Dorothy Gerosa*
*John and Barbara Bishop*
*With all my love*

# The SECRET of the NIGHT TRAIN

PARIS

# 1

# THE BEGINNING

Max Morel had never left France in her life. Now, on the first day of the Christmas holidays, she was sitting on the 3.55 train from Paris to Munich, a city in Germany.

It felt like a dream. An odd sort of dream. Max was sitting with her nose pressed to the window, wrapped in a warm navy coat and three scarves, accompanied by a nun who was humming to herself and fixing a shoe.

Why three scarves? Because December was bitter that year, and Max's mother had a great fear of the cold, and an even greater fear of far-away foreign cold.

Why the humming nun? That is a difficult question. Sister Marguerite is not really the sort of person to whom "Why?" applies. You will just have to put up with her.

And why was Max on the train at all? That is a much

easier question. She was going to visit her great-aunt Elodie in Istanbul. Or at least – that was the plan. But perhaps to *really* explain things, we need to begin with the day that Great-Aunt Elodie called.

# 2

# THE VERY BEGINNING

All Max knew about her great-aunt Elodie was that she had moved to Turkey years and years ago, and that she was very rich, and lived all by herself in Istanbul. Every Christmas she sent the Morels some well-meaning but ugly knitwear, and every year they sent *her* a card with a family photo printed on the front. Apart from that, they never heard from her. She hadn't been to visit since Max was a baby.

Then one day, when December had arrived and iced Paris all over with a slippery frosting, Max skidded-slid-stumbled home from school to find her mother on the phone. She was saying "Mm-hmm, of course" with her voice, and YOU ARE AN UNBEARABLE STRAIN ON MY SAINTLY PATIENCE with her eyes. The voice tinkling on the other end was not familiar. Max made herself some hot chocolate on the stove as usual, but extra slowly and quietly, so that she could listen for clues about the mystery caller. She was curious – this was out of the ordinary, and things at her house were hardly ever out of the ordinary.

After a very long time of "mm-hmm" and "of course", her mother finally said *au revoir*, and hung up the phone. She tutted, sucked in her cheeks and rolled her eyes all at once, which made her look like an overexcited prune.

Max tipped the steaming milk out into a bowl, and cupped the bowl tightly to get some warmth back into her fingers. "Who was that, *Maman*?"

"Your great-aunt," sighed her mother. "Is that *chocolat*, Maximilienne? Don't ruin your appetite for dinner, now." (She said this every day when Max made *chocolat*. Max's house was like that: most things happened the same way every day, like gently whirring clockwork.)

"Why was she calling?" Max asked.

Max's mother sighed a second time, even more gustily. "Your great-aunt," she declared, "is a very difficult woman."

This wasn't really an answer. Max was very curious

to know what made her great-aunt so difficult, but Max's mother started loudly tidying things that were already tidy, which was her way of letting Max know that she was asking too many questions. So Max took her hot chocolate, and some *tartine* to dip in it, and she went up through the house to the attic.

Max's house was full of thick curtains and dim lamps and soft carpets. It was a nice enough house, but a *heavy* sort of place. It was difficult to think anything new there, when everything was so sleepy and still and exactly-the-same-as-yesterday. Max had to find her own private places for thinking in. When she was small, she used to wriggle into a gap behind the sofa, but she couldn't fit there these days; so she had moved up into the attic instead.

No one else ever went up there. There was a skylight, and under the skylight there was an old red velvet chair that was too shabby for the rest of the house, and under the armchair there was a box of Max's notebooks. Today – like every day – she took out the latest notebook, rested the *chocolat* in the crook of her left arm, and began to write.

Max had been keeping notes for four years now.

They were notes about everything that happened each day – although with things being same-as-clockwork every day there wasn't always much to report, especially during the school holidays. Max's father said that she was doing Social History, and her notes could be very important in the Future. Max's older brother Pierre said she was being weird. Max's even older sister Claudette was much too old and important to have an opinion.

That day she made her notes, then sat and thought for a while, and watched the clouds shift over her skylight. The slice of sky above always made her feel like she could go anywhere and do anything. She forgot all about Great-Aunt Elodie's call until dinner.

The three Morel children and their parents always had dinner together, round a long table in a dark green dining room, with candles and all the right cutlery. Tonight, Max was imagining that it was the galley of a pirate ship to liven things up. She was the ship's captain, and they were going somewhere exciting, although she was a bit vague about where exactly. She gripped her sword (butter knife) fiercely, in case any of the other pirates were planning a mutiny.

"Your aunt Elodie called today," said Max's mother to Max's father. She made this sound as though it was *his* fault.

Max's father pulled a face. "What about?"

"Well, it's all very tiresome. Maximilienne, stop waving your butter knife around." Max made her fierce-sword-gripping a bit subtler, and Max's mother continued. "She's rather ill, and she has to have an operation. Apparently the doctor said she ought to have someone else at home while she recovers. She was asking if one of us would like to *visit*." She said "visit" as though visiting would involve wading through a large swamp, covering yourself in slime, and possibly wrestling with some ill-tempered crocodiles.

As far as Max was aware, though, Great-Aunt Elodie did not live in a swamp. She lived in a big and beautiful city, far away from Paris. Max forgot all about being a pirate captain sailing to somewhere-or-other. This was better: this was *real*. This was the sort of thing Max always *felt* might happen when she looked up through the skylight, but it never had – until now.

Her mother, however, was less excited. "I'm much too busy at work," she said. "And besides –" she turned to Max's father "– she's *your* aunt."

But Max's father had a very important meeting with very important people coming up, and couldn't possibly go, even if it *was* his aunt. Max's older brother Pierre had a national chess tournament that week, and Max's older sister Claudette had an international showjumping championship.

"Well, that's that, then," said Max's mother. "I'll just call her and tell her we can't go."

"I could go," said Max.

"She can't expect us to be at her beck and call," agreed Max's father. "We're very busy."

"I'm not busy," said Max.

"I'll just have to be firm," said Max's mother. "And we can all send her a get well soon card."

Sometimes, Max got the feeling that all the low ceilings and dim lamps and heavy curtains had cast a thick fog over her family, and they couldn't actually hear her. She tapped her mother on the shoulder. "*Maman*," she said, loudly, "it will be the Christmas holidays. I could go."

Max's mother and Max's father and Max's brother Pierre and Max's sister Claudette all turned to look at her, not sure what to do with this idea. Normal things for Max to do included going to school, disappearing into attics and being told off for daydreaming at the dinner table. Max going to Turkey to visit great-aunts was not on the list. Pierre snorted. Claudette examined her fingernails with magnificent disinterest.

"Don't be silly, Max," said her father. "You're only twelve."

Max was eleven, actually, but she decided not to point this out. "I'd be fine," she said. "It's not like I'd be staying by myself. I'd be with Great-Aunt Elodie."

"But it's so far *away*," said her mother. And she sighed despairingly at the thought of anyone being foolish enough to put a city so many miles from Paris. "It would be so tiring for you."

"I'd like to go," said Max. "Really." She tried to look sensible-and-reliable, while a great un-sensible balloon of excitement was being blown up inside her chest. To go all the way to Istanbul would be a hundred times more interesting than days and days of sitting in her attic and watching the sky and coming up with new things to pretend about the dining room. Maybe she would go on an *aeroplane*.

Pierre rolled his eyes. "You wouldn't like it. It won't be like one of your stupid games. You'd get homesick in three minutes."

"I wouldn't get homesick. I promise," said Max. "*Please* can I go?" And very subtly, just an inch, she turned her butter-knife sword on scurvy landlubber Pierre, who had already lost interest and was making a face at Claudette about something. Claudette, of course, was much too old and important to notice.

"We'll think about it," said her mother. And she started tidying the already-tidy salt and pepper shakers, so Max knew that she couldn't ask again. For the rest of dinner they talked about chess and showjumping and the neighbours, as usual; then they all had coffee and watched the evening news, as usual.

The headline was a new world record for the fastest solo hot-air balloon flight around the world. Max went to sleep that night imagining that she was flying a hot air balloon of her own, all the way to Istanbul, and her duvet was a nest of blankets in the bottom of the basket, and the on-off blink of the faulty street lamp outside was a star that she could navigate by.

"We'll think about it" was not normally a good sign. Max, however, was an optimist. She crossed her fingers all the way to school the next day; she had to uncross them to write, but she carried on pleading with the universe in her head, and doodled maps in maths and snaked tiny footprints all over her history book. At the end of the day she slid-skidded-stumbled home through the icy streets at top speed and went to her armchair to read about Turkey, and tug hopefully at her two long plaits, and look through the skylight, and generally wait for her parents to make up their minds.

"Please let them say yes," she begged the little slice of sky above her.

The little slice of sky wasn't bothered. A bird wheeled overhead, then went off somewhere else without her.

As things turned out, the universe *did* intervene on her behalf – or Sister Marguerite did, which felt like the same thing. Sister Marguerite played at Pierre's chess club. She was the only person who could beat him, which annoyed him a lot, but you aren't supposed to be annoyed with nuns so he had to be nice about it. When she heard the story, she offered to take Max herself.

"It's a stroke of luck," said Max's mother at dinner that night. "She spent some time in Istanbul when she was young, and she's keen to see it again. And she's a nun, so obviously she goes in for the whole charity thing."

"Isn't she a bit. . ." Max's father rubbed his beard, as if the right word might fall out of it – "odd?"

Max's mother pursed her lips, in a way that suggested that odd charitable chess-playing nuns were one of the trials of life, and she would rather not talk about it. "A little. But she's a *nun*. I'm sure she'll take good care of Maximilienne."

So, just like that, it was settled.

While Max fizzed with excitement, and had to be told not to *wriggle*, the others talked about chess and showjumping and the neighbours, and made coffee, and watched the evening news. Max found it difficult to concentrate. The headline was a break-in at a fancy vault in Paris, where lots of people locked away their diamonds and gold and so on. The police had turned up before anything could be stolen, which everyone on television

seemed very relieved about, but Max couldn't get very excited about diamonds that were so valuable you had to lock them away and not look at them. It would have been more exciting if they *had* been stolen. So she stopped listening, and thought about Istanbul instead.

What would it be like? And what would Great-Aunt Elodie be like?

She decided that she was probably going to like her great-aunt when a brown paper parcel arrived from her, sent by express delivery. It came on Saturday during breakfast. There was a letter on stiff headed paper saying how pleased Great-Aunt Elodie was, a picture postcard of Istanbul, a very ugly hand-knitted bobble hat ("For your travels across an Eastern European winter!") and two envelopes with tickets in. Max thought it was a friendly sort of parcel to send, even if the hat was a bit monstrous.

She opened up her packet of tickets, and was surprised to find four. She placed them in a line along the kitchen table. They were train tickets: from Paris to Munich, from Munich to Budapest, from Budapest to Bucharest, and from Bucharest to Istanbul.

"Are we going by train, then?" she asked.

Her mother sighed. "Your great-aunt doesn't trust aeroplanes, apparently."

Max couldn't help feeling that this was a bit beside the point, as her great-aunt was very much staying where she was. But she didn't protest. The trains sounded fun – two of them were overnight trains, and her mother explained that she would have a bunk to sleep in on board. And although she wouldn't have any time to explore Munich and Bucharest, she would have a whole day in Budapest. She looked up the cities in her atlas. Munich was in Germany. Budapest was in Hungary. Bucharest was in Romania. Max had heard of those places in geography, but she had no idea what they would look like. She whispered the names to herself.

Pierre was working on chess moves on the other side of the table, and he started glaring at her, so she scooped up her tickets and went to the attic to do her whispering there. As she left, Pierre was muttering that she was *way* too young and would *definitely* get homesick, but Max had learned that she could save a lot of time by not listening to Pierre. *Munich. Budapest. Bucharest. Istanbul.*

The next day she went to the library, and borrowed

every book about Munich-Budapest-Bucharest-Istanbul that she could find. The early darkness of winter evenings meant she did most of her reading by the light of a slightly broken lamp, as the attic didn't have an overhead light. She read about palaces and mosques and rivers and churches and lost kings and queens and battles. She read about the places in between, too, the places that the trains would pass through. She gave up making notes about her life in Paris, and made notes about the journey instead. This is the map she drew:

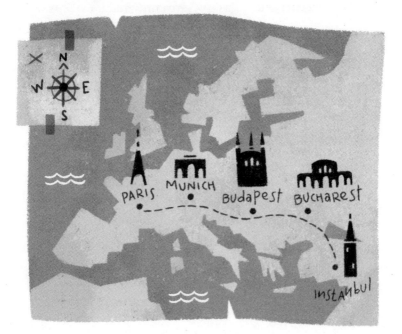

Even more than the places, she wanted to know about the trains, but they weren't in books. The train from Paris to Munich was in the newspapers, because it was new: a brand-new double-decker train, called the TGV Duplex. Max cut out the articles about it and stuck them next to her map. But for the other trains, she couldn't find out anything. She had hundreds of unanswered questions.

Her mother didn't know the answer to any of them, and her father wasn't much more useful, although he did try. "I learned something that might interest you, Maxie," he declared one evening. It was four sleeps before she was going to leave, and only her father was still listening to all her questions. "I was talking about your trip to a chap at work who likes trains, and he told me that the names of the trains all have meanings. I've written them all down." He pulled a note out of his pocket, with great satisfaction, and cleared his throat. "The Kálmán Imre – Munich to Budapest – was named after a Hungarian composer. The Budapest to Bucharest train, that's called the Ister; now that's the Latin name for the Danube River, which you'll cross. And –" he beamed "– the Bosfor train from Bucharest to Istanbul – now this is interesting – *Bosfor* is the Romanian word for the Bosphorus Strait, Istanbul's waterway." And he rubbed his beard in a pleased sort of way, like a Father Christmas who specializes in bringing useless facts to children.

"Oh," said Max, in her best interested voice. "Thanks, *Papa*. Did you ask him anything about what our carriages will be like? Or what we might see on the way?"

He had not asked this. He leaned back in his armchair with his eyes shut, well pleased with his contribution.

The days at school passed unbearably slowly. At last, there was only one more day of lessons, and then one sleep, and then it would be time to go. Max's mother gave her some money before she went to school that day, and told her to buy a case for her things on the way home.

This proved tricky. Max trailed around every bag shop she could find. There were huge suitcases and handbags and hiking rucksacks, but nothing quite right: they all seemed to belong to a different kind of person going on a different kind of journey. In the end she found exactly what she wanted by accident, in the window of a second-hand shop. It was an old-fashioned travelling case, small and brown, with metal clasps that *pinged* and a silky cream lining with a row of little pockets in the sides. It was a bit small, but Max was sure she could cram everything in.

She had some of her own money in her pocket for a new notebook, too. This was easier. She chose a pale blue one, and it was half price, so she also got herself a pen with smooth indigo ink.

By now it was getting late, and Max had promised not to be long, so she hurried home through the dark familiar streets. She said goodbyes as she ran: to the tree with a trunk like a face, to the shop with the best *pain au chocolat*, to her favourite house with its poppy-red shutters, to the distant Eiffel Tower that came in and out of sight as she ran, to her school playground and the post office and the cinema and the statue of an angel with the face all rubbed off.

As she raced round a corner into the Avenue de la Pompe, five minutes from her house, the soft street lamps were suddenly replaced by harsh blue light, flashing on and off. There was a cluster of police cars, and police offers were standing around importantly, and hurrying in and out of a grey hulk of a building. The building was just like all the others on the street, but it seemed somehow extra familiar – and then Max realized, with a shock, that it was the vault from the news, the one with the diamonds so important that they had to be locked away and not looked at.

She was very curious to know what was going on, but the way that the police officers were making notes and muttering into walkie-talkies reminded her of her mother tidying, and she thought she had better not ask questions. For a minute she lingered, trying to pick up clues, but a policewoman noticed and shooed her away. So she left the pulsing blue, and ran home double-fast to make up for lost time. There wasn't time for *chocolat* and the attic before dinner, so she scribbled her notes hastily at the kitchen table:

*Something going on again at the big vaults on*
*Avenue de la Pompe. Lots of police and everyone*

*looking very worried. A theft? No one would tell
me. I have bought a new brown travelling case
with creamy silk on the inside and tomorrow I
leave for ISTANBUL.*

While she was scribbling, her great-aunt called to
check that there were no problems, and to say again
how pleased she was, and to remind Max's mother to
make sure that Max had packed enough jumpers and
was definitely going to wear the horrible hat and had
snacks for the journey and so on. The tinkling of her
voice sounded kind.

Then there was dinner as usual, and coffee as usual,
and the evening news as usual, and at last it was time
to pack. Max packed her new notebook and her old
one, with the maps and notes on Munich-Budapest-
Bucharest-Istanbul. She packed her clothes and
washbag and hairbrush and the book she was reading.
She double-checked everything. Then she sat on the
edge of the bed, watching the street lamp outside her
window blink on and off, and she felt a bit peculiar.
She went downstairs to see what everyone else was up

to, but they were all busy preparing for meetings or studying chessboards or being-too-old-for-things, so she came back upstairs again. There was nothing else to do, so she changed into her pyjamas, and went to bed.

That night, she dreamt. The dreams were the messy sort that never really decide what they are about – she was running on and off trains, and trying to best a nun at an impossible game of chess, and searching everywhere for her red armchair in the attic, which always seemed to be just around the corner. Everything was washed in blue light, pulsing on and off, on and off. Eventually she woke herself up with worry, and by then it was dawn outside, and she was too hungry and alert to sleep again.

Suddenly, she was afraid to leave.

It was a feeling without words or shape, but it covered her all over, like being soaked in cold water. She missed her home, and she hadn't even left it yet. She missed the way that things happened at the same time every day, and she missed the heavy curtains and dim lamps and soft carpets, and she missed her own armchair with the skylight overhead.

Just lying there made the feeling worse, so she got up, put on her slippers, and went up to the attic. "I *want* to go," she told herself, "and I *won't* feel homesick." The sky outside was turning silver, and as she watched it lighten, she began to feel slightly steadier. "Munich," she whispered. "Budapest. Bucharest. Istanbul."

But by the time Sister Marguerite arrived, she was still feeling the strange cold-water fear. When she heard the doorbell, something inside her twisted sharply. She picked up her case and went downstairs to meet her chaperone.

To be honest, Sister Marguerite was not one hundred per cent reassuring. She somehow just *looked* like the sort of person who would always be tripping over things and missing trains and getting lost and so on. She was enormously tall, with miles of grey sock sticking out underneath her habit, and her wimple framed a long, lopsided face with an even longer nose. Max wasn't sure how you were meant to wear a wimple, but she was pretty sure that Sister Marguerite had got it wrong.

"This is Maximilienne," said Max's mother; and Marguerite broke into an enormous smile, as if Max was exactly what she had been hoping for.

"Of course she is! Ready to go, *mon lapin*?" (*Mon lapin* is French for "my rabbit", and it's quite a nice thing to call someone, if you happen to be French.)

Max nodded.

"Now, be good, Maximilienne," said her mother. "Remember, your great-aunt is very elderly. And she's not used to the Ways of Children." And she added a

third scarf to the two that Max was already wearing, and untangled the scarves from her plaits; which was her way of saying, "I love you, be safe."

"Goodness me," said Marguerite. "How alarming. I hope she's used to the Ways of Nuns."

Max's mother smiled politely, but it was wasted, because the nun was already marching towards the door in a billow of habit. She threw it open, and turned to salute Max's mother.

"Istanbul calling!" she announced. "*Au revoir,* Madame Morel!" And without waiting around for any further ado, she strode away down the street at a powerful speed.

Max gave her mother a hug goodbye, and reminded herself that it was exciting, and not terrible-and-horrifying, to be off on an adventure to Munich-Budapest-Bucharest-Istanbul. She took a deep breath, held on to her plaits, and scurried down the Rue de Vie after Sister Marguerite.

"Thought you weren't coming for a minute there," said Marguerite with a grin. "You OK? Got everything you need?"

"Yes, thanks."

"Incorrect, *mon lapin*," Marguerite declared triumphantly. "The first rule of travelling is: *you have always left something behind.*" And she chuckled to herself, as if this was a very good and unexpected joke.

They turned a corner, and Max's house was out of sight.

*Munich*, Max thought to steady herself. *Budapest. Bucharest. Istanbul.*

# 3

# PARIS TO MUNICH

An hour later Max and Sister Marguerite were sitting on the TGV Duplex train at the Gare de l'Est, Paris, waiting to set off for Munich Hauptbahnhof. The TGV Duplex was a double-decker train, and Max had a top-deck seat. From here, she watched as people heaved their suitcases up the platform, and hugged each other goodbye; and watched as latecomers pounded up to the train, red-faced and puffing; and watched as the platform emptied, leaving only an official in a bright orange jacket behind. Then she watched the emptiness for a long time, waiting for the train to pull out of the station. But it didn't. It was late.

Max still didn't feel right. Now that she was leaving Paris, she was all knotted up with a strange feeling – something a bit like being scared, and a bit like being sad, but not quite either of them. In her mind, Pierre rolled his eyes and said "I *told* you"; and Max tried imagining challenging him to a butter-knife duel across the dining-room table, but that made her think of home, and she felt even worse. She knew her *maman* was busy, but it would have been nice if she had been able to come and wave her off.

*I just have to think about something else*, she thought. *Just to get through the hard part.*

Sister Marguerite, meanwhile, had decided that now was a good time to fix her left shoe. She had produced a huge wood-handled leather needle and a bag of threads from her habit (along with two packets of crisps, a newspaper, a jar of jelly beans, and – Max tried not to stare – a houseplant for their table), selected a thick blue thread from the bag, taken off the shoe, and spent the last five minutes stabbing stitches through the leather and humming to herself. Max had a feeling that if she tapped her on the elbow and said, "I'm feeling a bit homesick," Marguerite would stop stitching at once and say something cheerful. But if she said that out loud, then Pierre would be proved right.

So Max pressed her nose to the window, and didn't

say anything. The minutes rolled on, and on, and still the train waited in the station. Passengers who had come in twos or threes muttered complaints to their friends, and passengers who had come alone raised their eyebrows at each other over the tops of books and newspapers. The muttering and eyebrow-raising grew and grew, and still the train didn't move. Back home it would be time for *chocolat* and notes, but Max couldn't have any *chocolat*, so she just got out her notebook. And that *did* make her feel a bit better.

She saw her entry from the day before, and picked up Sister Marguerite's newspaper, to see if she could solve the mystery of the police on the Avenue de la Pompe. She didn't have to look far: it had made the front page. While people around her muttered more and more at the delay, and her stomach did strange jumbling-abouts, Max tried to ignore it all and concentrate on the paper:

## "HEARTBREAK DIAMOND" STOLEN IN LATEST PHANTOM ATTACK

Police confirmed last night that they have discovered the theft of the so-called heartbreak diamond from a top-security vault in central Paris. A substitute "diamond" was left in the vault, and it is not known when the real diamond was removed. In a statement on behalf of the police force, Commandant Le Goff told the *Paris Gazette* that the theft is thought to be the work of the infamous "Phantoms".

The heartbreak diamond is only two inches in length, and shaped roughly like a heart. It is a red diamond, but divided exactly in the centre by a streak of white diamond. It is the only known case of such a jewel in the world.

The diamond's strange appearance is not the only reason for its romantic name. Legend has it that this diamond has never been owned by one person for more than three years without moving on. Some of its owners have lost the diamond to thieves, fires and floods; others lost their fortunes and were forced to sell; and one simply woke up to find the diamond gone. But the diamond's reputation as a heartbreaker has only increased its intrigue and value for jewel collectors.

This is the ninth high-profile theft by the so-called Phantoms. They have earned their name by stealing diamonds without damaging locks or breaking safes, as if they can pass through walls. Only one of their operations has ever been foiled, when German police intercepted phone conversations and were able to recover a valuable tiara.

The group are believed to operate from Istanbul. Police have advised that the diamond is likely to be transferred to their headquarters, and are working closely with the Turkish police to monitor all routes into the city.

True to form, the Phantoms have managed to steal the diamond without leaving a trace. "It's amazing," said Stephan Dupont, manager of Fort, the security firm in charge of the vaults. "I'm amazed."

"I'm really feeling a lot of amazement," he added.

M. Dupont went on to stress that the security of the vaults is "absolutely top class, top notch, top banana, seriously," and urged people not to panic. Nonetheless, jewel collectors across Europe are expressing grave concern for the safety of their prized possessions, and many are taking steps to move their most valuable jewels to new secret locations.

This is the second incident at the Fort Vaults this fortnight. Three masked robbers attacked the vaults last Wednesday, but were quickly apprehended before they were able to remove anything.

Max looked at the photo of the diamond, which seemed to wink from the page, as if it was pleased to have made its escape. Strange to think that it, too, was travelling to Istanbul. What sort of person, Max wondered, was a diamond thief? She tried imagining that *she* was a thief, the tiny diamond winking in her pocket while police hunted all over Paris.

And then, as if she had imagined them into life, there were police on the platform. They burst on to the cold grey emptiness quite suddenly, and fanned out, one to each door of the train. From Max's high-up seat they seemed to move silently, like shadows in their black uniforms. They were so exactly like Max's daydream that she felt her heart flutter nervously in her stomach, and she had to remind herself that they weren't *really* looking for her.

While most of the shadows guarded the train doors, three of them boarded, at the other end of the train to Max. She looked around the carriage: no one else had noticed. They were all too busy muttering and looking at their watches and putting up their eyebrows. But the next moment, the intercom crackled into life, and everybody stopped muttering and put their eyebrows down again to listen.

"Ladies and gentlemen," said the driver, "we are experiencing a slight delay."

"We know," muttered someone. A few people *shh*-ed him. They *shh*-ed so loudly that other people had to *shh* the *shh*-ers. There were a few seconds of general *shh* pandemonium.

"Police have reason to believe," the voice went on, "that a valuable object is being smuggled on this train. All bags will need to be inspected, and we must ask for your full cooperation. We may be here some time." The intercom crackled off, then back on again, and the driver added, "Sorry about that."

There was a froth of muttering up and down the carriage, as people agreed with each other that the driver did not sound nearly sorry *enough*. Max took her brown case out from under her feet and hugged it to her chest. A valuable item on board . . . *could* it be?

They were right at the far end of the train, and Max had to wait a long time for anything more to happen. The shadows guarding the doors never moved. While they waited Max and Marguerite got through most of the jelly beans the nun had brought, and Marguerite explained to Max all about how you sew the welt of a shoe to its sole, and they did half the crossword in the newspaper, and the muttering from the other passengers grew ever more mutinous.

At last, there was a *tut-PFFFfff* behind them. It sounded so much like a tut and a sigh that Max turned around, half-expecting to see her mother; but it was just the sound of the automatic door. And the person who came in was very much not her mother.

He was dressed in a smarter black uniform than the people on the platform, with a long black coat, and a face like a serious egg. Two ordinary officers stood behind him. He cleared his throat and held up a shiny badge.

"Police," he said, unnecessarily. "Bags, please." And he began walking up the carriage, inspecting bags and asking questions. The other two officers helped out by staring meaningfully at people, coughing importantly, and occasionally writing in notebooks.

Max stared at them. "What do you think they're looking for?" she whispered to Marguerite.

"Precisely what I would like to know, *mon lapin*," said Sister Marguerite, with enormous satisfaction. "We shall have to ask."

Max looked uncertainly at the serious-egg man, who was advancing up the aisle. He didn't look like the sort of person you were meant to ask questions. Something in the set of this man's jaw told her that uncertainties of any kind were not allowed anywhere near him.

But Sister Marguerite was not going to be put off by a firm jaw and a passing likeness to an egg.

"Good evening, *mon chou*," she said, as he approached their seats. "This is all very exciting. What are you looking for?"

*Mon chou* is French for "my cabbage". Surprisingly, it is actually quite a nice thing to call someone; but normally someone that you know very well, not stern police officers. The policeman's jaw got even firmer, and the other two officers stared very meaningfully indeed.

"A stolen item," he said stiffly. "I am Commandant Le Goff," he added, to avoid any more *chou* business.

"Bless you," said Sister Marguerite. "What kind of stolen item, exactly?"

"I'm afraid I'm not at liberty to say, Sister," said the Commandant, running an impatient hand through Marguerite's bag, then reaching out a hand for Max's. Max thought he seemed faintly bored by the whole situation. But if he was really Commandant Le Goff, then she had just read his name in the newspaper; and that just *might* mean that something very un-boring was under way.

She handed over her case, and decided that if Sister

Marguerite could ask questions, she could too. "Are you looking for the heartbreak diamond?" she asked.

Commandant Le Goff paused mid-reach, leaving his hand to flap around foolishly in mid-air. One of the officers started to nod, but the other one kicked him. "How – ahrrrrm," said Le Goff. "I am not at liberty to say."

"Oh, excellent guess, Max! Yes, I read all about that. It was in the papers," said Sister Marguerite, pointing at the newspaper on their table. The Commandant looked where she pointed, and raised his eyebrows at the houseplant, but didn't answer. By now he had recovered enough to take Max's case and start wafting his hand around in it. Max couldn't help thinking that if *she* was looking for stolen diamonds, she would do a slightly more thorough job. But Commandant Le Goff seemed keen to move on.

Marguerite was not giving in that easily. "How do you know it's on our little train, then?"

"We've had an anonymous tip-off. But I wouldn't get overexcited, madame. These people are normally time-wasters."

"Really?" said Sister Marguerite. "That seems a bit harsh. Surely we can be a *bit* excited. Will it go all the way to Istanbul by train, do you think?"

Commandant Le Goff snapped Max's case shut. "Good day, Sister. Good day, mademoiselle." The other two officers took their cue, and shuffled forward to stare meaningfully at the next row of people.

"Is that all?" Marguerite exclaimed. "The heartbreak diamond is tiny. I could be hiding it in my wimple."

The Commandant's egg face was starting to twitch a bit, as though it might hatch at any moment. "That will be all," he said. "Thank you."

"You don't want to double-check the wimple?"

"Really," said the Commandant irritably, "I think the wimple is neither here nor there." And he moved on to check the bags of nice, normal people who didn't bother him with questions and unusual headwear.

"Well," said Marguerite to Max, in a loud stage whisper, "I don't think that was very professional. I could be hiding half the Louvre in my shoes."

Max thought that this was unlikely, even in Marguerite's enormous shoes. But she was too busy watching Commandant Le Goff to object. He was scrambling hastily through the remaining bags, asking people vague questions and looking at his watch. He really didn't seem to be doing the job very thoroughly at all. He made it to the end of the carriage at top speed, thanked them for their time, announced that his junior officers would be staying on the train and should be alerted to anything suspicious, then ducked out of the carriage and off the train at double speed. As he hurried down the platform, the officers at the doors flocked after him. They were gone as swiftly as they had arrived.

The two officers left on board nodded importantly at everyone, and fiddled importantly with their hats. Then when that was done, they marched off importantly to fiddle with their hats in the other carriages as well.

Max scribbled all this down in her notebook, and twirled a plait as she thought it all over. "Sister," she began, "do you think there could really—" but then she was distracted by another *tut-PFFfff*. She thought Le Goff had come back. But the man who entered was very much not Le Goff.

He was a young man with flyaway hair, wearing a tweed jacket and the amazed smile of a man who is half an hour late for his train and finds it hasn't left the station yet. He made his way down the aisle, but did a terrible job of it, tripping over and bumping into everything available, squinting at all the seats as he went.

He stopped and had a really good squint at the pair opposite Max and Marguerite. "Excuse me," he said, "is this seat ninety-eight?"

"Seek and ye shall find," said Marguerite.

"Pardon?" The man's French had a heavy British accent.

"Yes," clarified Max, "it is."

"Magnificent news." The man put his bag on the rack overhead and folded himself into the seat. He fished into his pocket, and held up two halves of a pair of glasses, smiling ruefully. "Snapped them in London this morning. Absolute disaster. I waited ages on platform eight, only to find I was actually waiting on platform three. Piece of luck the train's delayed!"

"We had a police search. You missed all the fun,"

said Marguerite – raising her eyebrows at Max, as if to say, *conveniently*.

The man didn't notice, and kept smiling at a spot just to Marguerite's left. "Goodness, really?" he said, resting a casual arm on the table and accidentally knocking over the houseplant. Which, to be fair, Max thought, he could hardly have expected to be there. "Oh," he said, a bit confused, "sorry. Er – what was that?"

Sister Marguerite delved into her habit, produced a banana, tried again, and produced a small bottle of superglue. "Give those spectacles here," she said. "Let's get them fixed before you hurt yourself." And she waved the glue in his face, where he could see it.

"Heavens," the man exclaimed. "You are a star and a saint. Goodness! Piece of luck meeting you two! Now, what did I do with them?"

While he groped around in his pockets, the train gave a cough, and began to pull slowly out of the Gare de l'Est. As the changing view of Paris began to pick up speed, a knot in Max's stomach tightened violently, and she thought very hard about diamond thieves and mysteries to loosen it. Why wasn't the man out of breath like all the other latecomers? she thought to herself loudly. Had it really taken him *half an hour* to realize his mistake?

Outside the window, Parisian town houses began to give way to modern apartments, and the train was moving faster and faster. Max twizzled her plaits together and breathed deeply. But she felt worse than ever, as if without Paris to hold her together, she might just unravel completely.

So she imagined as hard as she could. She imagined that she had a long black coat like Le Goff's, and a stern face, and that she was on the trail of diamond thieves, and would never *dream* of feeling homesick. She imagined that she was secretly investigating this man, who had dodged the police inspection so neatly. Watching him carefully, she put on her best innocent face, and asked: "Sister, do you think the Phantoms are *really* on the train?"

"Phantoms have struck again, have they?" said the man. He *looked* casual. It was hard to tell when he couldn't meet your eyes properly.

"It's all over the papers, *mon poulet*." (*Poulet* is French for "chicken". Again, it's a nice thing to call someone. Maybe chickens are noble beasts in France.)

"If only I could read them!" said the man, gesturing to his glasses.

"Not long now." Marguerite pressed down on the frames, cross-eyed with concentration.

"You're an absolute star," said the man. "I'm Rupert, by the way. Rupert Nobes."

"Marguerite," said Marguerite, and "Max," said Max.

And then the announcement came on to welcome them to the train, and it was in German first, which Max didn't speak, and it was announcing stops that she had never heard of. *Think about something else*, she reminded herself. She stood up, with a swish of her imagined long black coat.

"Sister Marguerite," she said, "may I explore the train?"

Rupert looked a bit surprised, as if maybe it wasn't normal to want to explore a train that is the same all the way along. But Sister Marguerite just said, "Off you pop, find us something interesting," and swung her legs aside to let Max pass.

This was Max's plan:

Imagining being a detective wasn't enough to stop the unravelling feeling: she was going to have to really do some detecting to take her mind off things. And besides, she told herself, *somebody* ought to look properly. Le Goff had done the bare minimum, and if there had really been a tip-off that the diamond was on the train, then surely it was worth a little more investigation.

The first thing a detective needed was suspects. Rupert had to be Suspect Number One, because he had so neatly missed the police, but anyone with half a brain could have got past that inspection. That meant that *everyone* was a suspect, which was a bit overwhelming. But: if the thief was heading for Istanbul, they would make the same changes as Max and Marguerite. If Max could keep tabs on which of the passengers boarded the next train, that should narrow down the suspect list.

She just needed to know who was on *this* train first. She took her notebook out of her pocket, and turned to a blank page.

There were quite a lot of seats.

This was fine, because it was a seven-hour journey, and soon Paris suburbs were giving way all too fast to rolling fields and long thin trees, and Max was very happy to have a distraction. If she hadn't been feeling so jumbled up inside, it would have been fun. She had to be cunning: people don't appreciate you taking notes while staring at them, so she did a lot of wandering-up-and-down-looking-lost, and then darting into empty seats or tiny train toilets to scribble things down. She laid her pages out like the train carriage, and wrote down something unusual about everyone – like this:

| Red hat | Has tiny dog | | Green hair | Six earrings |
|---------|--------------|---|------------|--------------|
| Huge nose | Pointless sunglasses | AISLE | Triangular Face | REALLY TALL |
| Looks like Maman | Priest | | Dinosaur T-shirt | Glittery Nails |

At each stop, people left, and could be crossed off. "Red hat" and "Has tiny dog", for example, were gone at Strasbourg, and "Green hair" got off at Karlsruhe. The train really emptied out at Stuttgart: Max crossed off lots and lots of people, and made a little note next to Stuttgart on her map. By this time the two police officers had a lot less people to look importantly at, and as they tramped up and down, Max got the feeling that their hearts weren't really in it. Max, on the other hand, was starting to get excited. With so few people left on board, the idea of catching the thief suddenly seemed much more real.

She traced her finger along the line from Paris to Stuttgart. She had well and truly left France. It wasn't too bad on the warm bright train, speeding through the darkness. She only felt queasy when they pulled into train stations, dimly lit and alien, and she remembered that soon she would have to get back out again somewhere strange.

But then, each station also brought the fascination of finding out who would leave. By the time they pulled out of Augsburg, the stop before Munich, the train had almost emptied and her list had shortened dramatically.

There were several likely suspects on there, she thought. Her favourites were a fabulously well-dressed young woman in sunglasses; an elderly German lady in furs and jewels with a foghorn voice, who was travelling with a younger man built like a small mountain; two sharp businessmen with even sharper moustaches; and a bristled man in a raincoat clutching his suitcase very tightly. Some were so unlikely that she was almost tempted to cross them off – it probably wasn't the family with three toddlers, or the young couple reading poetry to each other – but she was a thorough detective, and she couldn't cross them off without good reason. After all, the thief could be hiding in plain sight by looking as ordinary as possible.

After her post-Augsburg headcount, she made her way back to her seat at last. *Rupert still here*, she thought. A lot of her favourite suspects were still on the train, in fact. The woman with the foghorn voice was still there, and as Max walked back to her own seat she was blaring angrily at the businessmen about something. The businessmen looked like they were trying not to cry. Max made a little note next to her: *slightly terrifying*.

"Find anything interesting?" said Sister Marguerite.

"Lots," said Max. Marguerite nodded approvingly. Rupert just snored gently – he was asleep, wonkily restored glasses back on his nose. Max had to admit that he didn't *look* like an international criminal.

Sister Marguerite started sweeping things back into her habit. "Get yourself ready, *mon lapin*," she said. "We're almost at Munich. Time for train number two!" And the driver came on and announced that this was the end of the line, all change, please, all change; and all around her the remaining passengers reached for their bags.

Max's stomach knot tightened. But she picked up her suitcase, and all the things that Sister Marguerite managed to forget (superglue, needle and thread, newspaper, empty jelly-bean jar). She wound her scarves tighter, and recited firmly to herself:

*Munich. Budapest. Bucharest. Istanbul.*

# 4

## MUNICH TO BUDAPEST

Stepping out at Munich was a lovely surprise, after all the dead, empty stations they had passed. It was just a huge grey barn, with none of the frills of the station in Paris, but it was bright and welcoming and busy – and there was *food*. Max hadn't realized how hungry she was.

"Right," said Sister Marguerite. "Just a couple of hours here, Max. Dinner!"

Max agreed wholeheartedly. But she dallied nonetheless, looking back over her shoulder as some of her suspects went through the exit and disappeared into the Munich night. She lost the fabulously well-dressed woman, which was a disappointment, and the sharp businessmen too. The two officers, duty done, left the train and trudged off to look importantly at some cups of coffee before returning to Paris.

They obviously hadn't seen anything suspicious. Maybe there was nothing to see. But Max would find out who got on the next train, at least; she was curious now.

The brightly lit food hall was decorated for Christmas, full of fake evergreen wreaths and wicker reindeer. Sister Marguerite steered them past a tempting pizza stall – "Germany, Max!" she declared. "Let's eat the most German thing we can find!" – and ordered something that sounded like a sneeze, but according to the sign was *schnitzel*. The man who sold them the schnitzel was friendly, and asked Max where she was from, in English. She knew a little bit of English from school. They managed a pretty good conversation, for two people speaking a second language.

She scanned the room. Rupert was here, talking to another of Max's suspects at the bar. She was a red-headed woman, covered in freckles, with a high forehead and flared nose that made Max think of a proud young dragon. Max had noticed her especially on the train because her eyes were different colours – one blue, one green. The effect was rather beautiful. Even from this distance Max could see that Rupert was doing a really terrible job of trying to impress her, smiling too much and laughing too long – and she was doing a really excellent job of ignoring him.

When they sat down with their *schnitzel*, which turned out to be a tasty sort of pork in breadcrumbs, Marguerite got the houseplant out again.

"Um. Sister," said Max.

"Yes?"

"What – er –" Max was looking for a subtle way to ask the question, but had to give up " – why do you have a houseplant with you?"

"A little keepsake, *mon lapin!*" said Marguerite, waving an enthusiastic fork. "It's from the convent. It's to stop me feeling homesick."

"Oh." Max considered this. "Does it work?"

"The right amount," said Marguerite. "I don't want to *not* be homesick. I like my home. But I don't want it to stop me going places. You do whatever you have to do to get past it." She pointed the fork at Max. "I know you've had the same trouble, *mon lapin*, and you're doing well. That notebook of yours – I don't know what you're writing, but it's working. Keep doing it."

Max nodded, wondering what Sister Marguerite would say if she knew that Max was writing a suspect list for her investigation into an international diamond-smuggling operation. "I will," she said.

After that Marguerite mostly told unlikely stories about the nuns in her convent, which were so funny that Max began to relax. Before she knew it, it was almost time to leave. Just for a few minutes, she stood at the front of the station, soaking up the crowds chattering in German and the lit-up restaurants and hotels and the wide roads and the bustle of Munich at night. The fresh air was steadying, and the mysterious sounds of German were exciting. Even though Max's stomach knot was still there, the balloon of excitement in her chest was back too, and they were in a tug of war inside her.

Sister Marguerite tapped her shoulder. "Come on, Max, we'll miss the train. You can have all day in Budapest tomorrow."

"I think I'll come back to Munich one day," said Max, yawning.

"Good plan," said Sister Marguerite, and she flapped

her habit encouragingly in the direction of the train. So Max took one last swallowing-up look at Munich, then followed her inside.

Max had expected that a sleeper train would be enormous, but the Kálmán Imre was very small indeed. A tiny corridor led to even tinier rooms, that Sister Marguerite called "couchette cars" – little rooms with six bunks for sleeping on ("They're called berths," said Marguerite, "like on a ship"). The berths folded out from the wall, a stack of three on each side, and could be turned back into seats again; there were straps at the side of the middle and top ones, to stop you falling out, and a pile of white sheets and brown rug waiting on each. The car was so small that only one person could stand in it at a time, so they all had to queue to stash away their luggage and make their beds, then lie down to make way for the next person.

Max was on a middle berth. There wasn't quite enough space to sit upright. She tucked her notebook under her pillow, wrapped herself up tightly in her brown rug, and watched as Sister Marguerite made a marvellous mess of putting sheets on the berth below.

"Are you finished yet?" barked a voice from behind.

The voice was speaking French, which was strange, because Max could have sworn it was the elderly German foghorn lady from the first train. Her voice was difficult to mistake. It was a thunderous croak, as though a frog had been given a megaphone.

"Just a moment," said Sister Marguerite cheerfully.

"There have already been moments," said the voice. "We have been here for so many moments that I can feel my skin wrinkling as I wait."

Sister Marguerite turned around to see the speaker, and accidentally (or was it?) spun the sheet as she twisted and somehow got it tangled up in her own habit. "Goodness," she said, "what active wrinkles you must have. I hardly ever notice mine. Oh *dear*, look what I've done."

Max craned round past her to see the speaker. It *was* the same woman. She had a remarkably triangular face – a perfectly normal forehead that ballooned out into a huge jaw – and below that she was a bundle of furs and jewels. Her elbows and knees stuck out to the sides, so that she walked in a sort of wide squat, which put Max in mind of a scuttling crab. In one hand she clutched a bag of pear drops, and in the other, a smart black walking stick, which she tapped against the ground with an impatient *click-click-click*.

Behind her loomed an enormous young man, his face squashed into a permanent expression of menace. Max was worried that he might turn that menace on Marguerite, but to her astonishment, he chuckled boyishly at her instead. "Let me help you there," he rumbled. Like the woman, his French was perfect, but they both had an accent that Max couldn't quite place.

"Thank you, Mr—"

"Grob. Klaus Grob. Call me Klaus. And this is Ester."

"Thank you, Klaus. I'm Sister Marguerite. This up here is Max."

Max waved from her berth.

"ARE YOU FINISHED YET?" croaked Ester.

"Nearly! Now, Klaus –" and Sister Marguerite paused mid-tuck, innocently, while an explosive tut erupted behind them "– is that a Swiss accent you've got?"

Of course! Switzerland has three official languages – German, French and Italian. That explained their

switch from German to French. Max hugged her rug a little tighter. If only all her investigations could be conducted lying here in bed.

"It is! Very good!" exclaimed Klaus, with genuine delight.

"But very irrelevant," added Ester, "to the task at hand."

"Here," said Klaus to Marguerite, smiling apologetically, "let me finish that for you." And he lifted Marguerite up by the elbows, put her in the corridor and whisked the sheets into place with a surprisingly deft touch, while chattering about where in Switzerland he was from; he had moved to Spiez recently, he said, but he grew up in Kandersteg, which is very pretty, oh! – lots of waterfalls and beautiful forests, you must visit it, best cheese in the whole country, very lovely people.

Sister Marguerite looked rather disappointed that her chance to cause mischief had been cut short, but she lay down on the bunk with good grace, and pulled a billowing pyjama-habit out of her bag. Klaus made up the other bottom bunk too, and lifted Ester up by her elbows and into her bed. "There you are, Ester," he said.

"Delightful," said Ester – but not like she meant it.

"What a treasure you are, Klaus," said Sister Marguerite. "How do you two know each other?"

"Ester is my aunt," said Klaus, stowing their luggage as he talked. "I'm taking her on a special holiday. She's always wanted to cross Europe by train. We spent some time in Paris first and we'll spend some time in Istanbul at the other end." He beamed. "It's wonderful. Slight mix-up with the tickets – we were meant to be in a private car – but otherwise it's all going brilliantly."

"Oh, how lovely!" said Marguerite. "How are you finding it, Ester?"

"Disappointing," hollered Ester, and she chucked a pear drop into her mouth and sucked at it noisily.

Klaus chuckled, said "Oh, *you*", and clambered up on to his berth with some knitting needles and wool. The berth sagged under his huge weight.

*So*, thought Max, *so*. That was two still on the list, and now they had names. Ester and Klaus. She couldn't make up her mind about Klaus: looking at his glowering face, she felt sure he had a history of terrible crime, but then he spoke and she sort of wanted to give him a hug. Ester, on the other hand, was cut-and-dried villainous. And *covered* in jewels. As she lay and thought, Max took out Marguerite's newspaper and superglue from her case, and carefully stuck the day's front page into her notebook.

The train began to slide out of the station, and Max sideways-watched Munich slip away. She couldn't see city or sky, just blackness dotted with lights. She still felt anxious, but it was helped by the cosiness of her berth, and the fascination of meeting two more suspects. Was Rupert on the train? Who else had come on board?

She found out when she went to brush her teeth. The train really was small. She only counted four people from the TGV: Ester, Klaus, the red-headed woman from the food hall, and Rupert Nobes.

"Hello there, Max," Rupert said, as she paused outside his car. "All right? Are you doing more of your exploring?" He had a middle berth too, and he had to curl his legs up to fit in it. He had taken his glasses off to read a battered old paperback, which made him look all vague and blinky again, and his hair was a bit tousled from the pillow.

"Just brushing my teeth," said Max.

"Good, excellent. Rather fun on here, isn't it? Like a sleepover!" he said, sitting up without thinking and banging his head on the berth above. "Bother," he said, and then added, "Oh, ow. Bother."

Next to Rupert's name, Max wrote, *Not sure he has it in him*. She decided to downgrade him from Suspect Number One, even if he *had* missed the inspection.

Back in her berth, she lay on her front with her notebook, and gave them each a page of their own: ESTER. KLAUS GROB. RUPERT NOBES. ? – RED-HAIRED WOMAN. Maybe they were just four innocent travellers. But looking at those four pages, her heart beat a little faster. After all, *somebody* had believed that the thief was travelling by train – believed it enough to tell the police – and if they *were*, then it had to be one of these four. That really wasn't too many suspects, and her half-game now didn't seem like a game at all. What if one of them really *was* the thief?

Everyone in her car was quiet. The only sounds were the click of knitting needles from Klaus's berth, and the steady thrum of the train.

A minute later the guard came to take their tickets, and their orders of orange juice or apple juice for the morning. Then he turned out the light, and slid shut the door on their car, so that Max could no longer see the city flashing past. The click of the knitting needles was gone now. The Kálmán Imre was settling down to sleep.

Max tossed and turned and turned and tossed, and her berth tilted with the movements of the train, and her thoughts wriggled about, and two hours later she was still awake. And thirsty, too. She had a water bottle in her case below. She didn't want to emerge from her blankets, but in the end she had to admit that she'd need a drink of water to get back to sleep. She tiptoed down the ladder.

Ester's suitcase was in the way of her own. She gave it a tug.

It was much heavier than she expected. She gave it another tug. She put both hands to it. She heaved. It shuffled begrudgingly forward.

She forgot all about the water, because her heart was

beating fast again. *Why* was Ester's case so heavy? From her berth nearby, the old lady snored. Max listened: everyone else seemed to be asleep too.

Max reminded herself that suitcases are private business. And she knew that this was what her *maman* would call "taking your games too far". But her *maman* wasn't there, and detectives had to look into private business sometimes, especially when there was a diamond thief on the loose – and there was no good innocent reason that Max could think of for an old lady's holiday suitcase to feel like a case full of rocks.

She opened the clasps.

It was disappointing. Layers of fussy silks and laces and old-lady underwear, and a huge stockpile of pear drops. She checked every zip pocket and shook out

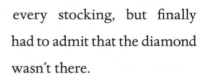 every stocking, but finally had to admit that the diamond wasn't there.

Now that she had started, she was too excited to stop. Klaus's

great grey case next. It whined gently as she unzipped it. Lots of soft balls of wool; some great Klaus-sized clothes; and an unnecessary number of socks. Nothing of note. Max had never really suspected Klaus anyway. But she was enjoying herself now, and she couldn't resist creeping to Rupert's car and checking his bag, since Le Goff never got the chance.

She opened the car door, *quietly*. She eased it shut again, *quietly*, leaving it open a crack to avoid the *thud* it made when you drew it all the way. She crept out into the corridor, *quietly*. And when she saw the red-headed woman glaring at her with her blue and green eyes, she even remembered to gasp quietly.

She turned the gasp into a yawn, and tried to stroll casually to the train toilet. The woman's eyes followed her the whole way, and when she came back out they were waiting, like two watchful night lights, seeing her back to bed. Max walked past as calmly as she could. Why was this woman lurking in the corridor in the middle of the night? What was she up to?

Back in bed, Max waited while the train made a night-time stop at a station, and there was a brief flurry of footsteps and voices. She tried to wait another hour at least, to avoid meeting the woman again. It felt like an eternity. But it was the sort of eternity that ends eventually, and when she peeked out again, the woman had gone. She was now even more curious about the woman than she was about Rupert. She tiptoed to her car, slid the door open, and listened.

"Hello?" she whispered.

Nothing.

There were only three people in here, and it was easy to pick out the woman's case – the other two were teenagers with hiking backpacks, covered in stickers from all round the world. The woman had a smart black case, and it opened with a surprisingly loud *ping*. Max *ssh*-ed it without thinking, remembered it was a suitcase, and felt a bit stupid.

The woman had what Max's *maman* would call "a tidy mind". Everything was immaculately folded and arranged. Spare clothes, a washbag, a hairbrush, a book. A stiff cream envelope, addressed to *Celeste Le Blanc, 17 Rue de Tarasque, Le Vésinet, France.* Max picked this up, examining the elegant swirling writing. It was very light – there couldn't be more than one sheet of paper in there. She squinted at the stamps in the almost-darkness. They were from Istanbul.

Max reminded herself that letters are private business – even more private than suitcases. But then she pointed out to herself that it might be a clue. She argued with herself for a while, but it was already beside the point, because she had started taking the letter out of the envelope the moment she had seen the stamps. She unfolded it, and knelt close to the crack in the sliding door to read it:

My dear Celeste,

I enclose a photo as promised. I look forward so eagerly to your arrival. Take great care, my dear! Never has a girl been more precious.

Yours,

M x

Max checked the envelope, but the photo wasn't there. Presumably it was tucked lovingly in a purse or a locket or something. Max was a bit disappointed.

Celeste hadn't seemed like she would carry photos around from people who called her a precious girl.

She reread the letter one more time. *Take great care*. Now that was odd. Why would Celeste need to take great care, if she was just on a normal train journey? Were she and her beloved M up to something dangerous?

She wrote *Take great care* on the woman's page, and added *Celeste Le Blanc* at the top. She realized she hadn't written anything for the others. *Weirdly heavy case, but couldn't see anything*, she wrote for Ester. The diamond was tiny anyway, she remembered – so, now she came to think of it, the heaviness was neither here nor there. After a moment's hesitation, she wrote *Who needs that many socks?* under Klaus. Which was a good question, but she couldn't see what socks had to do with international diamond-smuggling networks. She had to admit that it was a disappointing set of notes so far.

But there was still Rupert. The train was about to pull into a station again, so Max had to scurry back to her bed for a while until the thrum of the train had started up once more. In the corridor, she paused to look out at the night. There were no lights here. Were they in Germany now, or Hungary, or in between in Austria?

No way of knowing. Max's own ghostly face stared back at her from the window. She shivered, and got back to work, slipping silently into Rupert's car.

The car was full, and loud with the sound of six people sleeping. Max hardly dared breathe. Everyone had huge cases, and there wasn't quite enough room so Rupert had been forced to stuff his case at the bottom of his bed. It was very large, so he was almost folded double. Max eased it out very, very slowly.

Rupert snuffled, rolled over, bumped into the wall, and murmured some aggrieved English in his sleep.

Heart thumping, Max opened Rupert's case.

It was empty. No spare clothes. No toothbrush. Nothing. His jacket pocket held his tickets (Max checked: all the way to Istanbul), his passport, some money, his little paperback book, and his wonky spectacles.

Why travel with an empty suitcase? Surely that was odd? Max couldn't see how it helped, but it was strange enough to feel important. Better than Klaus's socks, anyway.

Rupert had started murmuring again, so Max crept back to her berth, and finished her notes under her rug. *Huge empty case*, she wrote, and after a moment's thought she added, *Leaving room for something?* But what? The diamond was tiny.

There was nothing more to do, but her heart was still pounding, as if she might somehow still get caught. She hugged her notebook closely, and ran over what she had seen in her mind, searching it for any missing clues. By the time her heart had slowed down and she began to drift off, there was a slight silver tinge around the edges of the curtain.

She was almost asleep when Sister Marguerite rolled over, sending the houseplant to the floor with a *thump*. Max's eyes jumped open.

*Sister Marguerite.*

Technically – *technically* – there should be one more name on her list of passengers that had boarded both trains. It did seem a bit unlikely. But then, everything about Sister Marguerite seemed a bit unlikely.

Max didn't want Sister Marguerite to be the thief. The thought set her homesickness off all over again. But the idea wouldn't let go of her. That is the trouble with ideas that you have before dawn: they are extra sticky.

She would have to just check, she decided, and then she could forget about it.

She crept down the ladder, pulled Sister Marguerite's bag out from under the bed, and put in a hand. Tickets. Money. Tissues. A book.

Of course, Le Goff had already checked the bag, but there was still the mysteriously endless habit. She folded it out, and checked its pockets. Crisps. The now-squishy banana. An umbrella. String. Flea spray. Mittens. Something cold and hard. . .

Max felt sick as she ran a finger along the cold-hard-something. That was definitely a gun.

She drew it out to take a look. It was a very dainty gun, small and pretty, but still very much a gun.

She rifled through the habit with more urgency. A pocket watch. A crossword book. A sheaf of notes, bound together with an elastic band. . .

They were brief letters. Max flipped through them, willing them to be innocent, but the evidence was stacked against her. *Fort operation will proceed as planned* – for a moment this meant nothing to Max, and then she remembered with a sinking heart that Fort was the name of the vault where the heartbreak diamond had been kept – *Next target will be HBD* – well, it was obvious what that stood for – and there, *Remove from Paris to HQ by train, 8th December, 3.55* – and there was a series of times and dates below. They matched Max and Marguerite's journey exactly.

Before Max could read any further, something was pressed just behind her ear.

"Stay where you are," hissed Sister Marguerite, "and don't move a *muscle* until I say you can."

**5**

# BREAKFAST IN BUDAPEST

Max froze. She waited to feel fear, and maybe see her life flash before her eyes. To her surprise, she mostly just felt sick with sadness. She had *liked* Sister Marguerite.

There was fumbling behind her, and then a small torch beam cut through the dark, into Max's eyes.

"Max?" said Marguerite. She lowered the cold-hard-something. That was the good news. The bad news was that Max could now see it was definitely the gun. She moved out of the torch's beam and looked at Marguerite, whose long face was drooping in horror.

"Max," she said, "I am *so* sorry. I didn't think—"

But before Max could know what she hadn't thought, Klaus's alarm clock was playing "The Sun Has Got His Hat On", and he was rolling over, creating a small berth-quake. Marguerite whisked the gun and the letters into her pyjama-habit.

"Good morning!" Klaus rumbled.

"Good morning, *mon chou*," said Sister Marguerite cheerily.

"Why is everyone *shouting*?" Ester creaked thunderously into her pillow.

Max should have said, "Help, help, she's a thief and she's got a gun." But she looked at Marguerite, her funny face looking naked and small without its wimple, and found herself saying, "Good morning."

Then the guard came round with their juice and croissants, and Max still didn't say "Help, help." She knew that she should, but something seemed to be sticking in her throat. Instead she picked at her croissant, then went to brush her teeth and collect her thoughts in the tiny train toilet. Celeste was at the window in the corridor again, staring out. Max wondered if she was thinking of the mysterious M.

She might have been *thinking* of M, but it was Rupert who appeared a moment later, smiling his best smile at her. His jumper was on back to front, and covered in croissant crumbs. Celeste stared outside harder than ever. Max left them to it. They seemed very far away, somehow: as though they were still on a nice safe train, where friends weren't thieves and nuns didn't carry hidden weapons, and Max was now somewhere else entirely.

Safely locked in the tiny toilet, she looked at herself in the mirror, trying to work out what she felt. She was somewhere in the middle of Hungary on a train and her only friend here had pointed a gun at her. What was she supposed to do now?

She stood like that for a while, but got no answer besides the thrumming of the train. All her homesickness had returned with such a rush that she thought she might *really* be sick, and the vibrating little room wasn't helping, so she stepped back outside. Sister Marguerite was there, clutching a bundle of habit and a washbag. She looked around, and then leaned in to Max.

"When we pull in," she muttered, "follow me lickety-split. I promise I'll explain, *mon lapin*."

And with that, she bustled into the toilet, looking for all the world like a nice nun in pyjamas, and not at all like a gun-wielding thief. Silver-gold fields rolled past sedately. Tales of guns in dark train carriages seemed silly now, somehow.

But it had been *real*.

When the time came to disembark five minutes later, Max was still so distracted that she managed to leave behind her case. That was how she came to meet Celeste Le Blanc. She felt a tap on her shoulder, and turned to see Celeste holding the case out, and smiling.

Max hadn't seen her smile before. She had small pointy teeth, which added to the dragon effect.

"You left this," she said. Her voice did not match her smile.

"Oh! Thank you."

"No problem. You want to be careful on these trains. Someone went through my bag last night."

"Oh!" Max said, twirling a plait casually. "Really?" She must have put things back too hastily in her excitement over the note. Of course Celeste would notice a disturbance in her so-tidy suitcase.

"Yes, really," said Celeste. "Luckily nothing went missing, but if I were you, I would be *very* careful." She

smiled her unwavering dragon smile at Max. Somehow, even though she had turned up the corners of her mouth, it felt more like she was snarling.

More to escape that smile than anything else, Max gabbled, "Oh, I've got to go, I'm going to lose Sister Marguerite," and ran off after the nun. Her heart was skittering about. She knew that she ought to be afraid of Sister Marguerite, but she found to her surprise that she was more afraid of Celeste.

When Marguerite turned and saw her, she broke

into a huge smile. "I thought you weren't going to come, *mon lapin*."

Max still wasn't sure if she *was* going to come. "Where are you going?"

They had reached the great arched entrance to Keleti station. Roads forked off in all directions, fanning out into the city. Max could see her breath in the cold air.

Sister Marguerite pointed to an ornate old building – actually, Max realized, *all* the buildings here were ornate and old – with a bakery tucked into the ground floor. "Breakfast," she said, "and a very good explanation. I promise."

Max considered this. Marguerite could hardly point a gun at her in the middle of the bakery. She could safely go for breakfast, and just hear what her former friend had to say. So she adjusted her three scarves, stepped out into the icy morning, and followed Sister Marguerite to breakfast.

Just crossing the road turned them both a glowing pink from the cold. Max understood now why her great-aunt had sent the hat, but Marguerite was hurrying ahead, so there was no time to stop and put it on.

Inside, Sister Marguerite plonked down with enormous satisfaction at a table for two by the window. "Perfect!" she announced. "I'm afraid we're going to have to have this conversation with one eye on the road, *mon lapin*. They've both gone for breakfast in the station, and I need to see when they leave – it's absolutely *crucial* that I don't lose them at this stage. But I owe you a private conversation."

Max didn't know what Marguerite was talking about, but this didn't seem to bother the nun. She groped around in her habit, never taking her eye off the station entrance, and found the houseplant for the table. Max wondered, with a chill, whether she had brushed past her gun on the way. The houseplant was followed by a crumpled bank note, which Marguerite handed to Max. Two thousand forints, it said, alongside a picture of an impressively bearded man. "Choose us something warm," said Sister Marguerite.

When Max came back with a plate piled high with hot pastries, Marguerite was still watching the road, still as a statue. Max followed her gaze. The cream stone front of Keleti station stared back. There was a small crowd outside, including Celeste, who was looking out across the city from a bench; and a lot of pigeons. No sign of Max's other suspects.

Not suspects any more, she reminded herself. She had found the thief. She was having breakfast with her.

"So the first thing you should know," said Marguerite, trying to take a pastry without looking and knocking over the salt instead, "is that I am very, very, *very* sorry about pointing a gun at you. I thought somebody dangerous was on to me, and possibly armed themselves; I never thought for the smallest second that it would be you. And between you and me, it isn't loaded." She successfully located a *kakaós csiga*, a "chocolate snail", and took a bite. "Generally," she said through her mouthful, "I find that you can have the same effect just waving the thing around and using a bit of cunning."

"But why do you need—"

"Getting to that!" Marguerite waved her *csiga* about in agitation. "We don't have much time, *mon lapin*, I must say all the important bits quickly. And you must listen just as quickly: ready?"

Max folded her arms and leaned back, to show that she wasn't anybody's *lapin* yet. But she nodded.

"Number one –" Marguerite held up one finger "– I am not the thief. Number two –" two fingers "– the thief is certainly travelling with us by train. And to explain how I know *that*, I should begin by telling you thing number three..." Three fingers, and then her hand dived back into her habit, and she produced a battered leather wallet. "Before I was a nun, Max, I was a commandant. And a much better one than that idiot Le Goff. I specialized in the international black market for diamonds and jewels."

Max picked up the wallet, and opened it. A younger Marguerite stared out, dressed in a shirt and with her hair scraped into a skew-whiff bun. The word POLICE was stamped below her in red, along with a lot of small print, and there was a shiny silver badge on the other half of the wallet. Max studied it suspiciously. It *looked* real.

"I wanted to carry on," sighed Marguerite. "But the police said they couldn't have a nun for a commandant, and the convent weren't too keen on having a commandant for a nun. I had to choose, so officially, I've given it up."

"And unofficially?" said Max. She looked from the policewoman to the nun, and back again. The same kink in the nose, the same amused twist to the mouth.

"Unofficially, I've been on the case of the Phantoms for a long time. I've still got connections all over the place, from my commandant days. A good friend of mine in Istanbul – his name's Salem, you can meet him when we get there, *mon lapin* – he was on the trail of one of them. Someone very low down the pecking order, we think, or possibly just a hired hand who didn't really know who she was working for. Anyway, she was mostly just on lowly errands, and one of them was to post those letters that you saw. Salem used to sneak into her house and make copies of them first, and post the copies to me. We think someone must have seen him getting away one night, though, because they stopped passing messages that way a few weeks ago.

"It's a very intriguing set-up. They must be paranoid about their phones being tapped, which is how their tiara heist was foiled a while back." Max remembered this from the paper, and made a mental note to underline this in her notebook. "It's a good system – the police aren't going to check every innocent-looking letter going out of Istanbul. But I've visited the house that the letters are addressed to, and it's empty, and no one ever shows up to collect the post. So why are the Phantoms sending letters that don't seem to be read by anyone? Now, *that's* a mystery, and if you can solve that, *mon lapin*, I'll buy you all the pastries you can eat.

"Anyway, as you saw, the letters told me that the diamond would be leaving Paris by train yesterday, and heading to Istanbul along our route. Clever idea. There's too much security on an aeroplane, but they're better off travelling in public if they can, instead of driving through the middle of nowhere. The *police* might not have a clue who they are, but you can bet that some other pretty nasty criminals are on to them, and they'd all like that diamond. Travel by train, and no one can surprise you in the middle of the night. Not as easily, anyway."

Max was sure by now that the police badge was real. It was flawless. And besides, it was just not possible to believe that Sister Marguerite was a liar. She chewed some *csiga*, and tried to hold all the new information together in her head.

She couldn't help feeling that they ought to tell someone what they knew. And then it occurred to her that maybe Sister Marguerite had already done that. "Were you the anonymous tip-off? You told the police?"

Marguerite nodded and spread her hands, as if to say *What's a nun to do?* "I tried, Max. But I was pretty sure that man was going to bungle it. He's useless. So I thought I'd better come too, and you gave me the perfect excuse. I was very stern with your *maman* about which day I wanted to leave. I got hold of a passenger list for the TGV – another useful friend – and based on that, I was sure that Rupert Nobes was our man. He's been up in court plenty of times for cons and theft, but they've never quite been able to pin it on him."

Of all the surprising information, this last piece surprised Max the most. "But he seems so. . ." she searched for the right word "– *useless*."

"Doesn't he just? Quite a disappointment in the flesh. Still, he's smarter than he looks." Sister Marguerite licked crumbs from her fingers. "But now, the catch. Ester Rosenkrantz wasn't on that list – she must have bought her ticket on the day. And that changes things. Ester's one of the most obsessive jewel collectors around. She doesn't have a criminal past *exactly*, but she's . . . ruthless. And she keeps her jewels at Fort, too, which might give her an opportunity. So, *mon lapin –*" and Sister Marguerite spread her hands "– Ester says she is on holiday with her nephew, and Rupert told me yesterday that he's going to visit a friend. Who's lying? Who is our thief?"

"What about Klaus?"

"Oh, he's new to me. I suppose we have to assume he might be working with Ester. But I rather like him."

"Me too," said Max. The balloon of excitement inside her was back, and swelling and swelling, and she had finally shaken off her homesickness. The game was *real* after all! And her friend was a real friend and not trying to kill her – which was a definite plus – and she was sitting in a brand-new city eating pastries with names that she couldn't pronounce, and the whole glowing day was ahead of her.

"There's one other person going all the way," she said, keen to show off her work. "Celeste Le Blanc." And she told Sister Marguerite about her night-time search, and the strange warning from "M". Marguerite looked impressed. She was still staring at Keleti station, so it looked as though she was impressed by the pigeons, but Max knew it was really for her.

"I'm glad you took a look, *mon lapin*," said Marguerite. "It was stupidly dangerous, but since you pulled it off, I'm glad." She knitted her fingers together and rested her chin on them thoughtfully. "Celeste's *probably* just in the wrong place at the wrong time – although the note is strange, I agree. I'll keep her in mind. But we can't tail all of them. Let's stick to Rupert and Ester: they've got history."

Max stared at her. "We're following people?"

"I was hoping so. I badly need some more information before we arrive at Istanbul." She did her best to look earnestly at Max without losing sight of the road. "Will you help me? It's up to you. I promise you can trust me, *mon lapin*."

Max looked out at Budapest, flooded with wintry light, and felt like she could go anywhere and do anything. "Yes," she said, "I'll help."

"Excellent," cried Sister Marguerite, pounding the table. She grinned. "Then you follow Ester Rosenkrantz. I'll take Rupert Nobes. Try and stay out of sight when you can, but don't let her lose you." She reached into her habit and put some more forint notes on the table. "Take these in case you need to pay to get in anywhere. Stick to her – you never know when she might reveal something crucial. And scribble down anything interesting she does in that notebook of yours."

Max folded up the forints and put them in her coat pocket. Suddenly, Sister Marguerite sat bolt upright and grabbed her arm. "Ester and Klaus!" she hissed.

Sure enough, the pair had appeared between the

cream pillars. Max could tell that Ester was talking, because pigeons were taking off left and right in alarm.

"There's your mark! Go, go, go!" said Marguerite, flapping her hands about in high excitement. Max hurried to her feet, untangling all her scarves from the chair and grabbing her case. She had a hundred more questions – some of them important ones, like, "If I lose them, how will I find my way back?" – but there was no time. She hurried to the door.

"Oh, and Max—"

"Yes?"

Sister Marguerite was still watching the road like a hawk. Or, thought Max, a sillier, stringier bird – an ostrich, maybe. But even if she was silly, she had turned out to be a friend after all – a friend and a detective and an adventure all rolled into one.

The nun gave her a thumbs up, without turning round. "Good luck."

# 6

## MAREK, MAREK AND RUSZY

Klaus and Ester paused outside the station, so that Ester could explain to a busker all the ways in which he was annoying her. Max waited for them behind a statue of a man-on-a-horse (it turned out that even in this strange new country, miles away from her own, all the statues were still of a man-on-a-horse), and while she waited she put on Great-Aunt Elodie's hat. It was warm and heavy, and when she tucked her plaits up inside it, it felt a bit like a disguise.

Then they were on their way, the busker left weeping into his violin behind them.

(Kind-hearted readers need not be too upset about the busker. He went home and put away his violin, which he never played again; but he took up gardening instead. He turned out to be very good, and won a lot of prizes. He even created a new kind of rose, and he called it *domine irasceris*, which is Latin for "angry lady", because he was so grateful to the woman who had terrified him into finding a new hobby.

His name was Erik, if you were wondering. Erik Filep.

But that is quite enough about Erik Filep. Ester and Klaus must not be let out of our sight: and they were, as I said, on their way.)

They set off down a busy main road. It was lined with buildings that looked to Max like huge fondant fancies – each a different pastel colour, and covered in curling stonework. They were beautiful. Surprisingly, they all had very ordinary shops on the ground floors, with lit-up flashing signs.

Klaus thought it was all *very* lovely, and kept exclaiming at everything, while Ester retreated further and further inside her furs in high grump. It was easy enough for Max to slip along behind them, blending in to the crowd, a shadow in a bobble hat. Ester could scuttle along surprisingly fast, but it helped that Klaus was about a foot taller than everyone else, so Max never really had to worry about losing them.

Things got trickier when they turned right, down a residential street. The pavement was empty, apart from a line of leafless trees, silver and silent. Max was neither silver nor silent (although she *was* leafless, I suppose), so the trees weren't much use for blending-in purposes. She hung back at the corner of the street, not wanting to get too close.

Her quarry came to a halt outside one of a terraced row of town houses. Klaus rang a doorbell. Ester rang it four more times, just to make sure, then banged on the door for good measure.

Max had to think quickly. Should she try and slip in behind them? But there was no way that she could do that unseen. She would have to try and talk her way in afterwards. Although, of course, she didn't speak any Hungarian.

The door opened, and Ester and Klaus vanished inside.

Max hurried along behind them, and looked at the building. It was a drab brown, like a moth between butterflies, and it had a silver plaque which read:

## 21 Téli Út

## Marek, Marek és Ruszy:

### Aukciósház

Then three more slim plaques, with a name each:

### Istvan Marek
### Daniel Marek
### Hanna Ruszy

Max didn't think that Marek, Marek and Ruszy, whoever they were, would just let in any old eleven-year-old, so she was going to need to pretend something to get through that door. She was good at pretending. Her plaits were not available for tugging, so she pulled at the bobble on her hat instead, and *thought*.

Then she knelt down on the pavement and opened her case. She took out Great-Aunt Elodie's parcel, which by now only contained the postcard and the letter (Max's tickets were in a pouch round her neck for safekeeping). She tore a page out of her notebook, and found the superglue that she had picked up when Sister

Marguerite left it behind. With that, she glued the parcel shut, glued the paper to the front to cover her address, and wrote on it: *Istvan Marek, 21 Téli Út, Budapest.*

She crossed her fingers, and rang the doorbell.

The door was opened by a small, neat man in a doorman's uniform, who made a small, neat "O" of surprise with his mouth when he saw Max, and frowned a small, neat frown as she pushed past him into the hallway.

The room was wood-panelled and dark, and smelled of polish and wealth. Along one wall there were three doors, and from the furthest away, Max could hear the tumultuous rumbles of Ester Rosenkrantz. There was another door at the end of the hall, and against the other wall were two wooden chairs, squatting under an oil painting of some deflated spaniels, and a hatstand.

Max sat on one of the chairs as haughtily as she could, and tried to look as polished and important as the hallway. The bobble of her hat fell forward with an undignified flump as she sat. She wished she had thought to take it off.

The man said something in Hungarian that sounded small and neat and quite annoyed. Which was fair enough. Max held out the parcel, and said firmly, "Istvan Marek."

The man reached out his hand to take it. Max couldn't let him do that. It was her only reason for being there.

"I have to give it to him myself. Very secret," she said, pressing a finger to her lips to make up for her meaningless French. She rubbed the tips of her fingers together, like a gangster talking about money. "Very valuable."

The man folded his arms, and unfolded them again, and tried folding up his forehead instead. He clearly wasn't sure how cross to be. On the one hand, people were not meant to turn up in this exclusive hallway uninvited and start playing charades with parcels. On the other hand, eleven-year-old girls with plaits spilling out of their bobble hats were not exactly the kind of nuisance he had been hired to keep out.

"He is busy," said the man, trying English to bridge their language gap.

Max sat up very straight in her chair. In her best English, she announced, "I wait."

Before the man could disagree, a phone rang from somewhere further down the hall. The man looked towards the ringing. He looked at Max. He looked at the ringing again. He did a little shifty dance of confusion. The phone call was obviously important.

He made up his mind. "Wait there," he said. And he tapped away down the hall with small, neat, very hasty steps.

As soon as he was gone, Max was across the hallway, and had one ear to the third door.

A sign proclaimed that it was the office of ISTVAN MAREK himself. Istvan's voice was breathy and soft, barely dribbling through the door. Ester was loud and clear. At first Max assumed that they were speaking Hungarian, but the words were sort of smoother round the edges than the Hungarian she had heard, and she realized as she listened that they too were using English. There was a clicking noise just to the left of the door; she guessed that Klaus had been left to sit and knit while they talked.

She got out her notebook. She wished her English was better: she could only understand the odd word.

Even so, she could tell that Ester was not happy about something. More not happy than usual. Every time Istvan Marek said something soft and reasonable, there was an answering thump of Ester pounding some unseen furniture, and her voice would get a notch louder.

Max scribbled down what she could understand. There was "much too cheap", and "very good price", and the word "stupid" a lot. She strained to hear more. Was Ester trying to sell something? Could it be *the* diamond? If so, it didn't sound like they were going to reach an agreement.

Voices in the room rose – Ester sounded by now as not-pleased as it was possible to be – and then Max made the important discovery that Istvan Marek's office door opened outwards. She discovered this because Ester shoved it open without warning, and sent her flying.

She landed with a thud, which was followed by two medium-sized thuds and a large one: Max knocked over the hatstand, Ester tripped over the heap of hatstand-and-Max, and Klaus tripped over the heap of Ester-and-hatstand-and-Max. Max didn't know the word that Klaus rumbled in German, but she was pretty sure it wasn't polite.

By the sounds of things, Daniel Marek and Hanna Ruszy then joined Istvan in the hallway to see what all the thudding was. It occurred to Max, as she lay with her face squashed into Marek, Marek and Ruszy's expensive green carpet, that this probably wasn't the most secret a secret investigation had ever been.

But it also occurred to her, as she listened to Ester clambering to her feet with an almighty roar, that with her face in the carpet and her hat over her hair and her body half covered by the contents of the hatstand, they probably didn't recognize her. Yet. So she lay face down, and prayed that they would leave quickly.

Thankfully, Ester was not someone who concerned herself with why other people might be lying around on carpets. As far as she was concerned, that was just the infuriating sort of thing that Other People did. She hurled a hurricane of outraged English at Marek, Marek and Ruszy, and the universe in general; then she stormed to the door dramatically, her walking stick click-click-clicking.

Klaus was more of a problem. He crouched down at Max's side. "OK?" he asked. "OK?"

"*Klaus*," bellowed Ester. And Klaus sighed, stood, and followed Ester to the door. The dramatic-storming-out was now slightly ruined, so Ester had to slam the door twice as hard to make the point.

Above Max, the doorman was rapidly explaining something in Hungarian. Presumably, the *something* was the presence of a small bobble-hatted Ester-trap lying in the hall.

Max had to get out of there before she lost Ester and Klaus, and was left stranded in some unknown corner of Budapest. She sat up. Three long, thin, silver-haired people peered down at her, swaying slightly, like riverside reeds perturbed by a strong wind. The doorman hovered anxiously behind them.

"Istvan Marek," Max explained, standing and shoving the letter at the man nearest Istvan's office. She made for the front door. But one of the reed people – the woman, so it had to be Hanna Ruszy – clamped surprisingly strong hands on her shoulders. Max wriggled, but with no luck.

The doorman must have told them she was French, because it was in French that the third of them – Daniel Marek – began to scold Max. Like Istvan, his voice was thin and breathy. The other two didn't look like they were following the French, but they swayed about angrily in support of his general sentiment.

"Do you have any idea," Daniel breathed, "who that *was?*"

"Sorry," said Max, "but I've really got to—"

"Ester Rosenkrantz! The most important client who is ever likely to call on us." The others sighed a rippling sigh at Ester's name.

"Sorry," Max repeated, "really. Could I just—"

"Oh," wheezed Daniel, his pale face reddening, "She's *sorry*. She's outraged the richest woman in Switzerland, the only child of *the* Karl Rosenkrantz, the heiress of his entire fortune, the most wanted client of jewel dealers around the world, who will probably now never cross our threshold again, but if she's *sorry*—"

Istvan murmured something soothing to Daniel

in Hungarian, a hand on his arm. Daniel took a huge breath, and his red face began to return to a more normal colour. They all swayed gently. Clearly, Marek, Marek and Ruszy were not used to feeling this much emotion in one go.

Hanna's hands were still gripping on to Max's shoulders.

"Please," said Max, "could I—"

But she didn't have to finish the sentence, because Istvan was looking at the contents of the parcel, and something that he said sharply to the other two made them both forget her for a moment. Hanna lifted her hands as she reached out for the letter.

Cover blown: now they all knew that she hadn't brought a proper parcel at all, just a letter in French and a postcard. They were going to want to know what she was doing there. Max would guess she had about three seconds before she was in really serious trouble.

She ran.

They shouted huskily after her, but she was already slamming the door, pounding down the street the way she had come, praying that Ester and Klaus would be in sight. The bright sky and stinging cold were a shock after the warm, lamplit hallway.

At the end of the road, she looked left. Cars and colourful curling buildings and trees and twisting black lampposts and crowds of people and pigeons and no sign of anyone she knew.

She looked right. Cars and colourful curling buildings and trees and –

– and very far off, but helpfully a foot above everyone else, the looming head of Klaus Grob. Max laughed out loud with relief, and sprinted after them, weaving in between the crowds. It was wonderful to be back outside, heart pumping, leaving those three long, silvery people to sway about by themselves in their silent hallway.

As she closed in on her quarry, she slowed to a jog, and her heart began to calm down, and her thoughts began to fall into place. And as she dropped to a walk, following them past a park that had turned forlornly brown for the winter, she noticed that one of her thoughts felt particularly niggly. And then she realized why.

This was what she realized:

If Ester Rosenkrantz was the only child of this Karl Rosenkrantz person, then she didn't have any brothers or sisters. And if she didn't have any brothers or sisters, then she couldn't have any nieces or nephews. And if she didn't have any nieces or nephews, *who was Klaus Grob*?

# 7

## THE SZÉCHENYI BATHS

Ester and Klaus, whoever they were, marched onwards. Max followed. They kept up a fast pace, and it was hard work, but the pleasure of finding her first proper clue pushed her on. Surely, if these two were lying about Klaus, they *must* be up to no good.

At the edge of the park they came to an enormous ice rink, speckled with figures in bright jackets who criss-crossed over it in sweeping arcs. A bridge over the ice led them to an old castle at the side of the rink, sprouting turrets with peaked red caps, and at its gate there was a cluster of wooden huts selling hot food and heady spiced wine. They stopped. Lunch.

Max was starving: lunchtime had been and gone ages ago. She bought something doughy and warm and covered in cheese from one of the huts. Clutching her paper bag, she retreated to a picnic table that was right next to Ester and Klaus, but hidden behind a large tree. She could hear Ester loud and clear; above her, a squirrel was hiding under its own tail in alarm.

Ester was complaining about something in German, and Max couldn't follow at all. So she took the opportunity to update her notebook. On Ester's page she wrote:

*Visiting Istvan Marek. Who? Why? What was she trying to sell?*

And on Klaus's she wrote:

*Ester Rosenkrantz is an only child. Klaus claims to be her nephew. Who is he really? Why is he lying?*

She was lost in her thoughts for a while, until quite suddenly there was a frenzied croaking from the other side of the tree, and Ester went scuttling away at a startling speed across the grass. Max peered around the tree trunk to see what had happened, and saw Klaus trying to encourage an enormous spider on to his hands. The spider was not impressed. It hurried away across the table, looking quite a lot like Ester.

Even when Klaus had managed to get rid of the spider, Ester refused to return to the table. She was shaking and croaking gently to herself. Sighing, Klaus returned to the table to pick up both their cases and Ester's bag of pear drops, and went off to comfort her.

Then they were off again, and Max had to scoop up her notebook and trot after them.

It was only as she left that she noticed Celeste. She was sitting at another picnic table, a little way off, staring into the distance. As usual. Max watched her, waiting for a sign of life. Why was she always just sitting around staring? That was something that people in films did, but not real people with brains to get bored and fingers to get cold. What was she up to?

A moment later Rupert appeared, too, clutching two plastic beakers of something steaming hot, trying to wave at Celeste and splashing half of one beaker down his coat. Max glanced around for Marguerite, but her friend was well hidden.

Strange, Max thought as she trotted after her quarry, that everyone was together on this unimportant patch of grass. If most of them were innocent bystanders, why were they all drawn to each other like that? She had the uneasy sensation that they were all being knotted together, in ways she couldn't see. But she *would* see, in the end, she was sure. She slipped her detective's notebook carefully back into her pocket.

They hadn't gone far when Ester and Klaus arrived at a round building coated in butter-yellow paint, iced with looping white stone, like an enormous birthday cake. Max didn't need any clever tricks to get inside this one. The double doors were wide open.

Inside was a large entrance hall with a black-and-white marble floor. In here, Ester's click-click-click was hugely magnified, and Klaus's footsteps sounded more enormous than ever. Max hovered at the door as the two of them went over to a woman behind a glass screen and paid her some forints. Then they disappeared through another set of double doors.

Max hurried over to the woman. A sign said *Széchenyi*, followed by a list of mysterious words and prices, but that didn't really help. So Max just put down the largest forint note she had, and smiled hopefully. When smiling hopefully got no response, she tried holding up one finger. "Um," she said, "one, please?"

This did the trick. The woman pushed back a mountain of change, and a blue plastic wristband. "*Úszóruha?*" she asked – and pointed at a rack of swimming costumes to her right.

This didn't *seem* like a swimming pool. It was much too grand. But Max thought she had better have one, for whatever-it-was, if that was the done thing. She picked out one in strawberry red, remembered she was a secret detective, and changed it for a more forgettable navy. She pushed the change-mountain back to the woman again, who rolled her eyes, took a single coin off the top, and pushed it back. Then the woman handed Max a thick white towel, and waved her away at last. Max went through the double doors.

She had thought that the building looked like a birthday cake, but now she saw that it was more like a doughnut. She was in a ring of corridor, and through windows she could see that the heart of the ring was outdoors. She peered out. It was full of people, but they were clouded by a thin mist that seemed to cling to the place. She realized that she was looking at a glittering blue pool; the air was so cold that where it met the water, the water was shocked into swirls of vapour, creating the mist.

It was an outdoor pool, in December, in Budapest. Max shivered, and wished she had been given Rupert Nobes to follow. She was sure that he wasn't doing anything this stupid.

But there was nothing for it: she changed into her costume, crammed her things into a locker, thought warm thoughts, and dashed through the freezing air to the waiting mist and icy blue.

To her surprise and delight, it was warm – gloriously warm – and full of unexpected *bubbles*. Every inch of her body sighed in relief. The pool wasn't really a swimming pool: she could stand in it, and people were just lounging around enjoying the bubbles and chatting. It was more like one of those Roman baths she had studied at school. She cut through the water, trying to find Ester and Klaus in amongst the mist, pretending to be a submarine with just her eyes above the water.

She found Ester sitting by herself. She was squatting at one wall of the baths, eyes closed, a blissful smile smeared across her enormous jaw. Max knew how she felt. She turned a somersault through the bubbles, and they rippled and swirled around her, and she didn't think her body had ever felt this light and content.

But where was Klaus?

A small tidal wave answered her, knocking her sideways midway through her second somersault, and sweeping two elderly ladies away to the far side of the baths. Klaus had arrived. He was wearing bright orange trunks and a blissful smile, and he splooshed joyfully in the water.

*"Guten tag!"* he cried.

But Ester was not on board with *guten tag*. For reasons that Max couldn't comprehend, she was furious with Klaus. Her angry torrent of German scared off everyone that hadn't been washed away by his tidal wave, leaving an empty semicircle of fury around the two of them. Ester was turning a reddish purple, and surrounded by the swirling mist, she looked terrifying.

Max bobbed at the edge of the semicircle, hidden by the mist. Why was Ester angry that Klaus was here? Did this hold any clues to who he really was?

Klaus was trying to reason with Ester, but this was

like trying to reason with a hurricane. She was heaving herself up and out of the baths, and once she was out she stamped and screamed, and screamed and stamped, pointing to the door. Trying to make Klaus leave.

Klaus sank deeper into the bubbles and mist, looking *almost* sulky.

Ester was attracting attention. A worried lifeguard tried to plead with her to calm down, but she snapped at him so viciously that he whimpered and hurried back inside, skidding on the wet floor as he ran. He returned a minute later looking smug and much less whimpery, with a large man in black behind him: security. When Klaus saw this, his sulky expression hardened into something more menacing, and he heaved his body out of the bubbles to go and stand by Ester.

As his shoulders rose out of the mist, Max noticed a tattoo: a line of arrowheads, black then red, then black then red, snaking angrily across his left shoulder. It wasn't a pretty tattoo. Somehow, it made her feel uneasy. She sank back deeper into the comforting bubbles.

The security man was large, but Klaus was larger. A lot larger.

If Klaus alarmed the security man, he didn't let it show. He said lots of calm and sensible Hungarian, with lots of calm and sensible nodding of his head. Ester blared over him in German. He raised his voice. Ester blared over him some more. He went to put a heavy hand on Ester's shoulder.

Quick as lightning, Klaus's hand was on his wrist, restraining him. The security man opened his mouth to object. Then he saw what the twist of Klaus's arm had revealed: the tattoo on his shoulder.

He turned very pale. He apologized and lowered his arm. He murmured some more soft apologies, shuffling his feet. And, just like that, he left.

Max wallowed about uncertainly in the water. What did *that* mean? Was it something to do with the tattoo? If not, what else could have changed his mind?

That was the end of the argument, and the end of Max's blissful time in the bubbles, because Ester and Klaus stamped off together to the changing rooms. Max sighed, and decided to allow herself three more somersaults before she got out. She could change faster than them anyway. All right, five more somersaults.

Maybe six.

Twelve somersaults later she pushed herself out into the cold air, found her locker, changed hastily, and hurried to wait outside the front doors, tucked out of sight behind a tree. She waited. She waited. She shivered as the cold air clung about her wet hair. She waited.

She did some more waiting, while she wondered about who Klaus Grob really was, and why the security guard had been so afraid of him.

The sky was starting to darken. Max checked her watch. It was really time to be getting back to the train station.

For the first time since she had set out into the bright Budapest day, the knot in her stomach started to retie itself. This wasn't Paris. The streets were strange and unfamiliar, and there was no one who would understand her if she asked for directions, and she didn't know where you could go to find out information or get a map. If Ester and Klaus had left before her, what was she going to do?

Five minutes later, they still hadn't appeared, and hot tears were pricking at Max's eyes. She checked her watch again, even though she knew what time it was: late. Almost too late. They must have already left. She tried to ask a passing woman where the train station was, but the woman couldn't understand her, and when Max started miming a train, complete with desperate chugging noises, she hurried off in alarm.

"What *are* you doing?" said a voice behind Max – in sweet, glorious French. Max spun round to find Celeste watching her, eyebrows raised.

"Oh!" cried Max, breathless with relief. "Hi! I'm lost. You're going to the train station, right? Can I come with you?"

Celeste didn't answer, but she began walking down the path, and seemed to expect Max to follow. So Max hurried after her.

"What are you doing here?" Celeste asked, without looking round.

Once again, Max seemed to have angered her, although she couldn't think why. "Um. Swimming."

"Without your guardian? And without knowing how to get back to the station?"

"Um," said Max, "I thought I knew. But I got confused."

"You seem to be quite careless," said Celeste. She made it sound as if Max's carelessness was a crime against her personally. Or, maybe, as if she didn't believe it was carelessness.

"Sorry," said Max.

There was silence all the way to the edge of the park.

"I'm Max," said Max.

"OK," said Celeste. She did not offer her name, so Max had to go on pretending not to know it.

"I'm going to Istanbul," Max added, "to visit my great-aunt." (Which was true enough, but seemed like a very distant idea now – Max couldn't imagine arriving at the other end, and being polite and making small talk over dinner and so on.)

Celeste didn't even bother with an "OK" to that, so Max gave in. She was too tired to worry much about investigating Celeste. She was their least likely suspect anyway, Marguerite had said; and Max's head was as full as she could manage already.

As they walked, Budapest continued to darken around them, and the street lamps were turned on.

Celeste kept up a furiously fast pace, and Max had to half run to keep up.

It seemed almost surprising, after she had done and seen so much, that the station should be waiting where she left it, so unruffled and calm. The cream stone looked majestic against the darkening sky, and the windows glowed a gentle gold. She had made it. When they went inside, they found the train already waiting for them on platform six.

*Bucharest*, thought Max, suddenly exhausted. *Bucharest, Istanbul.*

# 8

## BUDAPEST TO BUCHAREST

The Ister was almost empty when Max boarded, and it was still almost empty when it pulled out into the inky dark. She and Sister Marguerite had a couchette car to themselves.

What with the long day, her sleepless night and the soothing rhythm of the train, Max was struggling to keep her eyes open, but she had to swap notes with Marguerite before they could sleep. She wolfed down the sandwiches Marguerite had bought, and recited everything she had seen.

"Magnificent work, *mon lapin*," said Marguerite, lacing her fingers together and propping up her chin, which Max was now noticing she did whenever she was thinking hard. "You've done brilliantly. That tattoo of Klaus's. Describe it carefully?"

Max described the angry red-and-black tattoo on

Klaus's shoulder.

"Hm. That's the mark of *Die Eiserne Hand* – the Iron Hand. Self-styled 'security experts' – they're just a gang of thugs for hire. Vicious lot."

Max stared at Marguerite. She was suddenly rather glad that her friend was carrying a gun, and began to wish that it *was* loaded after all.

"So," said Marguerite brusquely, as if she shared trains with vicious gang members every day, "Klaus is not Ester's nephew, and he's an Iron Hand. And Ester tried to sell something today – Marek, Marek and Ruszy are auctioneers, and rather shady ones too. Not above dealing in stolen goods on the sly. This is *excellent* work, Max."

Max never knew what to say to compliments, so she just looped a plait around her ear, and said, "What about Rupert?"

Sister Marguerite sighed. "Total washout. He spent the whole day mooning around after that Celeste woman, trying to casually bump into her, finding ways to impress her. Like a lovesick puppy! If he *did* have criminal intentions when he got on this train, he's clearly decided that they're not as important as this schoolboy crush. I think maybe he *is* just on holiday." She stitched her fingers together harder than ever. "The one that interests me now, though, is Celeste. At first I couldn't work out what she was doing. She spent all day just wandering at random and waiting outside buildings and staring. But I began to see what was happening, and now I've heard how your day went, I *know* I'm right. Celeste spent the day following Ester and Klaus."

"What? *Why?*"

"Precisely the question I would like answered," agreed Sister Marguerite. "I don't like it. I don't know what her game is. And whatever it is, Max, I'm afraid she will almost certainly have noticed that you were *also* following Ester."

Max's heart skittered again, thinking of Celeste's dragon smile. What was she up to? For a while the two of them sat in silence, thinking, while the Ister slid through the darkness. Then Marguerite stood up abruptly, and pulled the curtains shut.

"Bed," she said. "I might not be the most conventional guardian in the world, but I can still enforce bedtime."

And she shooed Max off the seats, and began turning them into berths. "Go on, go and get our bedding. It's in the guard's room this time. At the end of the train."

So Max pottered down to the guard, and picked up two packs of bedding. She paused on the way back to lean her forehead on the cold glass of a corridor window and think about what she had learned. It was hard to adjust to Klaus as a violent gang member. And why was Celeste mixed up with them? And had she, Max, got tangled up in it now too?

The window was open at the top, and there was an icy draught on the back of her neck. The train had stopped at its first station; an electric light picked out the sign, which proclaimed they were in SZOLNOK. Nothing moved in the frozen night. For a minute there was just cold, and peace.

Then Max saw a shadowy figure cross the platform. It was Rupert. He walked right up close to her window, and for a moment Max thought he had come to talk to her. She almost waved. But then he stopped a foot away, under a ghostly overhead light, and she realized that he was by a payphone – it was a red phone mounted on a platform pillar, with a plastic shell above and around it. He stepped under the shell. Max ducked down out of sight and waited, hardly breathing, determined not to miss a word.

Whoever picked up spoke first, and at length. Max knew because there was an eternity of uninterrupted silence before Rupert was allowed to speak. Thankfully, his English was clipped and clear, and Max could mostly follow.

"I said I'd call. I keep my promises. I'm sorry I'm late – there wasn't time at Budapest."

A shorter silence.

"No. Not yet."

A medium-sized silence. Max peeked over the edge of the window. Rupert was hidden by the shell, only his legs showing. His trousers were too short. "There's no need for that," he said. He sounded much less vague than usual, and strained. "No need. Be reasonable. I'm telling you I'll get it."

There was another pause, and then Rupert half shouted *"Please—"* but the unknown caller must have hung up, because a moment later he slammed down the receiver. Max heard the sound of footsteps hurrying back to the train, and – loud in the Szolnok silence – one sharp, gulping sob.

The sob was so sad that she very nearly ran to Rupert's car to see if he was OK. She only just stopped herself in time. However upset he was, he was still a suspect – and she needed time to think about what that phone call might mean. Hugging the bedding close to her chest, she hurried to tell Sister Marguerite what she had heard.

But when she returned, Ester Rosenkrantz and Klaus Grob were in their car.

"Klaus snores," Ester was announcing. "I'm sleeping here."

Klaus smiled apologetically. "It's true. Runs in the family. My great-great-uncle snored competitively. Won a lot of medals for Switzerland."

"Why this car?" asked Marguerite bluntly.

"Next door to mine," said Ester. "I want to be near my nephew."

Max and Marguerite both snorted sceptically at the same time. There was a second's awkward silence, interrupted by a loud thrum as the train started up again.

"Make my berth, Klaus," Ester ordered. "I'm tired."

And so Max couldn't tell Marguerite anything, and had to lie down on her berth with the whole day bottled up inside her, listening to Ester sucking on her pear drops and smacking her lips.

Her mind whirred, keeping her awake. She got out her notebook and updated her suspect pages, which helped. When she had finished, they read:

? - ~~RED-HEADED LADY~~

### CELESTE LE BLANC

"Take great care". Who is M? Why is he writing to
Celeste, and why should she take great care?

Are they up to something?

Following Ester and Klaus?! Why?


### ESTER ROSENKRANTZ

Weirdly heavy case, but couldn't see anything.

Jewel collector. Keeps her diamonds at
Fort Vaults.

Visiting Istvan Marek. Why? What was she trying
to sell?


### KLAUS GROB

Who needs that many socks?

Ester Rosenkrantz an only child. Klaus claims
to be her nephew. Who is he really? Why are
they lying?

UPDATE: Member of Die Eiserne Hand. Here as
Ester's security? Why didn't she want him to
join her in the baths?

RUPERT NOBES

Late to the train – missed police search. Blamed
    his snapped glasses.
Huge empty bag. Leaving room for something?
Known con man!
Strange phone call. Promised he would have
    something for somebody. Sounded upset.


Max tucked away the notebook, and tried to banish the images of the day from her mind. She kept seeing the fear on the security guard's face, and the fury in Celeste's smile. For the first time, she felt the weight of what they were doing. Was she getting caught up in more than she could handle?

The Ister was chillier than the Kálmán Imre, and Max tucked her blankets tightly around herself. It had been a long day, and she had hardly slept the night before. Despite her worries, she fell straight to sleep.

She was woken up again by a loud *thump*.

Or, she thought as her mind began working properly, maybe she had dreamt a *thump* and then woken up. It was difficult to be sure. Either way, she didn't know what time it was or where in the world the Ister was by now, and she was in that night-time haze where nothing seems quite real, and there was a strange sense of dread in the pit of her stomach. If it *had* been a dream, it had been about something awful.

Now that she was awake, she needed the toilet too badly to just drift back to sleep. She poked a cautious foot out of the blanket. It was freezing. She poked the rest of herself out of the blanket very reluctantly.

As she crept down the dimly lit corridor, something about that *thump* lingered in her mind. She hurried to the toilet double-quick and hurried double-double-quick back again – but as she passed Rupert's door she paused, remembering his desperate phone call, suddenly overcome with pity for him. His door was open, rattling slightly as the train swayed along. She peeked inside.

Rupert wasn't there.

He had turned his seats into a berth, and made up the bedding. It gaped in the darkness like an empty mouth, the blanket lolling over one side like a tongue. As the train sped past electric lights the car flashed light-dark, light-dark, reminding Max of the blue lights outside Fort Vaults. Her unease seemed to thicken. What was Rupert doing, creeping around at night?

Somewhere further down the train a door banged, snapping Max back to her senses, and she hurried to bed before Rupert could come back and ask what she was doing. She slept, but she dreamt uneasily all night.

In the morning there was snow.

Now, I don't know how much snow you have seen in one go, but you probably need to picture more snow than that. There was a flat sheet of snow stretching all the way out to the horizon, finally meeting far-off mountains covered in more snow. Only the very tallest mountains had snow-free peaks, and they stood out against the winter sky like bruises. Sometimes the train passed fir trees iced all over with snow, and every now and then they passed houses oozing icicles from the eaves – houses with football posts and picnic tables, monuments to a summer that was now impossible to imagine.

Sister Marguerite woke up to see Max with her nose pressed to the window, and smiled. "Welcome," she said sleepily, "to Romania, *mon lapin*."

Ester Rosenkrantz had got up before either of them woke, and they found her in the restaurant car, tucking into an enormous breakfast. Klaus was opposite her, breakfast finished already, knitting needles in hand. Celeste arrived only moments after Max and Marguerite, and sat down with a book. It was almost a complete set of suspects: only Rupert was missing. There were some strangers in there too, mostly half asleep, clutching coffees and tackling piles of breakfast. Max just ordered a hot chocolate. She wasn't really hungry. And besides, she hadn't gone this long without *chocolat* in years.

"No food? None of my delicious food?" said the Romanian man in charge of the car. He was round-faced and ruddy, with a permanent smile, and spoke to Max in English. "It is very good. I guarantee!"

"No, thanks," said Max, smiling to make up for her lack of Romanian and her limited English.

"With that smile," declared the man, "I forgive you! Some people in this car do not have smiles." He glared over at Ester, who chewed steadily on her breakfast as if butter wouldn't melt in her mouth. "Sadness! I will not have people bring sadness into my restaurant car. We shall have some happiness." And he turned on a radio, which he apparently thought would bring happiness. A poundingly cheerful pop song played. Ester turned a violent shade of purple, Celeste pointedly held her book even closer to her face, and even Klaus looked a bit pained.

Max joined Sister Marguerite at their table, where the houseplant was already in place. Marguerite was tapping her foot in time as if she, at least, was quite enjoying the radio.

With one last flourishing key change, the song finally ended, and a serious Romanian voice came on and told them the news.

Marguerite smiled at Max. "Did you sleep well, *mon lapin?*"

Max stirred her hot chocolate. "Kind of."

Marguerite leaned closer. "You are quite safe," she whispered. "I promise. I am taking care of you."

"Thanks," said Max. And she did feel a little better. Outside, the snow twinkled merrily at her, as if it was on their side as well.

There was a clatter behind them. The chef had

dropped a plate of toast, and was staring at the radio in horror. At the smash of plate-on-floor, everyone turned to look. The man kept staring.

"Everything all right, *mon poulet*?" Sister Marguerite asked him.

A rapid exchange of English followed, that Max couldn't keep up with. Marguerite's face drooped in horror, and she fired back urgent questions. Celeste seemed able to follow, and listened wide-eyed. Ester and Klaus continued eating, unconcerned.

"What was it?" said Max, when the chef had bustled out of the room, muttering worriedly to himself.

Marguerite had turned very white. "A man was found by the side of the train tracks," she said. "There was some sort of accident. He fell from the Ister last night."

The hot chocolate in Max's mouth suddenly felt sticky and cloying. "Rupert?" she whispered.

"It's hard to be sure. The description was a bit vague. But brown eyes, brown hair, middling height – it could be him. I haven't seen him this morning. He wasn't in his car when I passed."

"And he wasn't in his bed last night," said Max. She felt sure it was him. She was remembering the sickening *thump*. "What did they say happened? How do you just *accidentally fall* off a train?"

"In my opinion," said Marguerite, too quietly for anyone else to hear, "it would be difficult without some help." And behind the houseplant, she made a little pushing motion with her hands, to show Max what she meant.

Max thought of the threatening phone call she had overheard, and felt sick. "Is he. . .?" She didn't want to finish the question.

"He's alive. Luckily. It's a miracle anyone found him. Lying in a snowdrift. A few more hours. . ." Marguerite stared at the passing snow, and left the sentence lying between them, limp and unfinished. Max shuddered.

She looked at Celeste, Ester and Klaus. Who would push Rupert? Celeste, annoyed with his attention? Or, she thought, *or*, had he *really* been following Ester and Klaus? Did that phone call last night hold any clues?

She felt awful. She knew it didn't make sense, but she couldn't help feeling that she might have stopped it, if she had been able to tell Marguerite what she'd heard. The memory of his choked-back sob played on repeat in her head.

Klaus tapped Sister Marguerite's shoulder, knocking her slightly off balance. Under his furious eyebrows, his eyes had widened. "Sorry," he said, "I couldn't help overhearing. Someone has fallen from the train?"

Max nodded, watching Klaus. He *looked* upset.

"We think," said Marguerite shakily, "that it was the young British man who has been with us since Paris."

"Oh!" exclaimed Klaus. "In the tweed? Yes, I remember him! Rupert, wasn't it? Remember him, Ester?"

"No!" declared Ester.

"Excuse me," Celeste cut in.

All of them turned in mild astonishment to Celeste. It was not like her to volunteer to speak. A stranger came sleepily into the restaurant car, took one look at the shattered crockery and the unlikely collection of faces gawping at Celeste, and left in haste.

"What makes you think the man was Rupert?" Celeste asked. She was staring icily at Sister Marguerite.

"Well," said Marguerite, "the description. . ."

"The description was very ordinary," said Celeste, with uncharacteristic passion. Under her freckles, her face had flushed. "Every second man fits that description. They didn't even say that the man who fell was British. Why would you assume that it was Rupert?"

That wasn't easy for Max to answer, as the answer was "Because we know that someone on this train is smuggling a diamond to Istanbul, and Rupert is one of our suspects, and I eavesdropped on his phone call yesterday so I know that someone is threatening him, and then I was snooping around in the middle of the night after I heard a loud thump and I snuck into Rupert's room and saw that it was empty"; and that didn't seem like something she should just announce to everyone over breakfast. There was a longish pause. The radio had moved on to an angsty ballad with lots of dramatic drum rolls.

"Look, Celeste," began Sister Marguerite, in her best reasonable voice, "we're all feeling – OW!"

Max had kicked her under the table, but it was too late. Celeste's eyes had widened in shock; then she rearranged her face into its usual empty stare, snatched up her novel, and swept out of the carriage.

"What?" said Marguerite, rubbing her shin. "What did I do?"

Max was trying to find a way of silently explaining, but it was a difficult sort of thing to mime. How would *you* say, without words: *We haven't actually been introduced, so neither of us is supposed to know Celeste's name?*

As it turned out, Max didn't need to explain, because Klaus did the job for her. Well – sort of.

"Oh dear, she's taken it hard. Oh, poor man. What awful news," he said. He had hunched his shoulders as small as they would go, and was doing a good imitation of shock and sorrow, but Max could not forget the arrowheads marching across those shoulders under his shirt. After a hunched, sad little pause, Klaus started knitting again, and said casually, "Why did you call her Celeste?" – and there was a moment of penny-dropping on Sister Marguerite's face, before Klaus confused things, by adding, "Her name's Suzanne."

At that, Marguerite was firmly back to confusion

again, and this time Max joined her. She made a small beard of confusion out of her plaits. "What? I thought her name was Celeste Le Blanc?"

"Nope," said Klaus firmly. "I chatted to her on the last train. I like to get to know my fellow passengers." He paused his needles a moment to tick off all the things that he had learned on his fingers: "Suzanne Leroy, works at the post office in Paris, lives with her boyfriend Paul, two cats and a parrot." He smiled, pleased with his findings, and resumed knitting.

Max twizzled her plait-beard. Paul? Then who was M? Did it matter anyway, if M had been writing to another woman entirely? She tried to hold all of it straight in her head, but the memory of Rupert's phone conversation kept getting in the way and making it difficult to think straight.

"Now, Max," said Klaus. Max could tell that he was doing that motherly voice, where you sound extra cheerful and extra sensible to make everyone feel better. He pointed a needle at her. "I haven't really talked to *you* yet. Report for duty! Full name? Where are you heading? Spill the beans!"

"Max Morel," said Max. "I'm going to Istanbul to visit my great-aunt Elodie." And she stared pointedly out of the window, to make it clear that she didn't want to be cheered up, and she wasn't going to talk any more. They were up in the mountains now, chugging through dense fir forests. Trees filled their windows, snowy branches pawing at the carriage as they rushed past. Max felt much too hot.

Ester had been silent throughout the whole episode, chewing and glaring, but at Max's words her head rose up out of her furs.

"Elodie Morel?" she hollered. "You're related to Elodie Morel?"

Despite herself, Max looked around at that. "Yes," she said. "Do you know her?"

"Yes!" Ester gave the table an enthusiastic slap. "I knew her back when she was still Elodie Yavuz, before her Mr Yavuz popped his clogs. Haven't seen her for *years*, though. The last time must have been – oh – the Berlin auction of '67. I had no idea she'd changed her name back to Morel."

"Berlin?" Marguerite echoed. "'67?"

"Yes." The table got another good slap. "Absolutely unbearable woman. She outbid me on the Bamberg Crystal Penguin. Well, well. Elodie Morel's great-niece."

Max looked from Marguerite to Ester, and back again. Marguerite was staring at Ester as though she was seeing her properly for the first time.

"Excuse me, *mon chou*," she said, "I'm feeling rather unwell. I might just have a quick lie-down." And her eyes flickered briefly to Max, and Max knew with absolute certainty that "lie-down" meant "follow a hunch about Ester Rosenkrantz". Her heart quickened. She tried to look concerned about Sister Marguerite's health, but her face went all jumpy, and she couldn't remember how she was supposed to arrange it.

Marguerite's look had unsettled her. If it had been anyone else, Max would have said that she looked afraid.

As Marguerite bustled out of the breakfast car, Klaus stood, and was with her in two enormous strides. "Here," he said, tucking a huge arm around her, "lean on me a bit. You *are* looking peaky. Do you feel faint?"

"Thank you, Klaus, but I'm quite all right. Don't worry yourself."

"Nonsense! I'm seeing you safely to bed. You've gone pale. . ." And Klaus steered Marguerite through the door, arm still clamped around her, refusing to be brushed off. The door slid shut behind them, shuddering as it banged into place.

Ester looked at Max. Max looked at Ester.

"Well, well," said Ester, "Elodie Morel's great-niece. What a small world!" She licked her lips, chasing the last of her breakfast, and settled back down into her furs.

Outside, snow began to tumble from the sky, covering up the tracks, smothering everything it touched.

**9**

# BUCHAREST TO ISTANBUL

Klaus was a suspiciously attentive nurse. When they pulled into Bucharest Nord, he was still at Sister Marguerite's berth-side, clicking away at his endless knitting and telling her gentle-stories-to-cheer-up-an-invalid. Even when Max arrived to "look after her", he wouldn't go. He insisted on helping her off the train.

"Let's get you some sweet tea," he said firmly, once they were all on the platform.

To be fair to him, Marguerite *was* looking pale.

"No need," she said, extra firmly. "I'm going to find the ladies' toilets." This was a small victory: Klaus couldn't see a way to go with her, although he insisted on seeing her to the door.

Max was going to follow and find out what Marguerite was thinking, but Celeste sailed in ahead of them, so they still couldn't talk privately. Instead,

Marguerite handed her some crumpled Romanian money – leu. "We've only got fifteen more minutes before the Bosfor," she said. "Get us some lunch, *mon lapin*, and we'll talk on the train."

Never had the word "talk" sounded weightier. "Talk" staggered out of Marguerite's mouth, carrying the load of all the morning's revelations, and of all the thoughts she was keeping to herself... But Klaus was still standing there beaming and remarking on the weather, so for now Marguerite just squeezed Max's hand and disappeared down spiral steps to the toilets.

"Too cold for my taste," Klaus concluded, "but *so* beautiful."

"You shouldn't be so happy," Max snapped. "A man fell off our train. It's *bad*." And she stomped off to get lunch, leaving Klaus looking crestfallen.

Bucharest Nord was wide and grey, opening out on to a row of tracks that cut black curves through the snow, stretching out to the horizon.

Any other time, Max would have longed to explore. Now she barely even saw it. Rupert gone. Celeste possibly called Suzanne. Ester a friend – or, rather, rival – of her own great-aunt. And *what* had Sister Marguerite realized about Ester?

The Bosfor was already waiting for them. Max found her seat in a daze, and sat nose-to-window. It was strange to think that it was less than two days since she had sat like this on the TGV, just a girl feeling a bit homesick.

She was homesick again. At that moment, she would have given a hundred heartbreak diamonds for her own red armchair at the top of her own house. The memory of that chair was so overwhelming, so much more real than anything around her, that it took her a moment to realize the sickening, terrible thing that was happening. When she did realize, she nearly cried out.

The Bosfor was moving.

The Bosfor was moving, and Sister Marguerite was not in her seat.

They picked up speed. Bucharest Nord rushed away from them as the Bosfor pulled out, and out, and out, on unstoppably to Istanbul.

*She's probably just sitting in the wrong seat,* Max told herself. But even though she was an optimist, there was a great yawning pit in her gut, because she didn't believe that at all. She hurried up the train, scanning all the cars, praying for a glimpse of crumpled wimple, of long grey sock. She hurried back down again. She did that twice more, as if she might somehow have failed to notice the world's tallest nun. Then she sat back down in her seat, and cried.

There was one other person in her car, a lady dressed all over in a powdery purple. She half smiled, half frowned at Max in a concerned bid to be kind, and said something in a soothing voice. Max couldn't understand her – she was speaking Turkish – but it wouldn't have made any difference, unless she happened to be saying, "Don't worry, Sister Marguerite has not been hurt by whoever pushed Rupert off the train, and they will not be hurting you either, and everyone is safe, and I have got your red velvet armchair here for you." And she probably wasn't saying that.

For the first time, Max didn't care *who* it was who'd stolen the diamond, and pushed Rupert, and vanished Sister Marguerite. She just wanted them to stop.

But she realized, as she took some gulping-great

breaths, that knowing who they were truly mattered now. She didn't know what they had done to keep Sister Marguerite from the train, but she had to find out, and somehow make things all right again. Marguerite had promised to keep Max safe, but Marguerite was gone. It was up to Max.

So she took some more of the gulping breaths, held on to her plaits, and *thought*.

What had Sister Marguerite realized? Ester knew Great-Aunt Elodie, and had visited Berlin, to bid for a crystal penguin. What had that told her?

And what had she left the restaurant car to look for? Something in their sleeping car – which had also become Ester's sleeping car. Whatever it was, Klaus Grob – Die Eiserne Hand security – had put himself firmly in the way. Max would bet the heartbreak diamond itself that the answer was waiting in Ester Rosenkrantz's luggage. She would have to take another look. And the sooner the better. She didn't fancy sneaking about at night, when anyone could be waiting for her in the shadows, ready to get rid of another nuisance. She would go now.

But how to distract Ester and Klaus? She needed an idea, and fast, but she was still having trouble thinking in straight lines.

The woman opposite her had been rummaging in her handbag, and she finally produced a cookie, with great triumph. She wafted it kindly at Max. Max did her best to explain, via head shaking, how extraordinarily useless a cookie would be at that moment. Her throat tightened with sadness. The woman was so kind, and so ordinary, and so unlikely to bother herself with diamond thieves on trains. Max missed Marguerite painfully.

When they rumbled over the Danube River, leaving Romania behind and crossing into Bulgaria, she still hadn't come up with an idea. Gradually they left the snow, and chugged past valleys stiff with frost, and swollen black streams, and *still* she didn't have an idea. Even though she was an optimist, her hope wobbled.

The sky began to spit rain, and the drops raced each other down the window. A spider crawled ponderously across the pane.

And that was when Max found that she *did* have an idea, after all.

She tried putting her hand in front of the spider, but this spider knew a human hand when he saw one. He crouched stubbornly still every time she went near him. So Max tore a page from her notebook, took Sister Marguerite's jelly-bean jar from her suitcase, cupped it over him, and took him by surprise from underneath with the paper. He waved a leg in feeble protest.

"Sorry," Max said. "If it helps, I know how you feel."

The powder-purple lady was now truly worried about her. Max smiled reassuringly – or as reassuringly as she could manage, with a face smudged from crying and a trapped spider in her hands – then she set off down the corridor once more.

Celeste was at the window, staring out, as usual.

Ester and Klaus's car was in the next carriage, thankfully, away from Celeste's gaze. Max cupped the jar to the crack at the bottom of the door, and slid away the paper.

"Good luck," she whispered.

The spider spidered off, not bothered. Spiders do not really worry about *good luck* and *bad luck*. For spiders, the world is just made up of *flies* and *not-flies*.

Max backed off into the corridor of her own carriage, and watched through the window, trying to look casual for Celeste's benefit. For a while there was only the sound of a baby crying, and the usual train-rattle.

Just when she began to think that the spider must have threaded itself into a nook somewhere unseen, there was an enormous roar, followed by some very high-pitched croaking. Double-quick, Ester was pelting down the corridor to the next carriage over. Klaus was in close pursuit. The door to the carriage slammed behind them.

Quickly and silently, Max entered the carriage from the other end, and slipped into their car.

The suitcase was stored under a seat. Max heaved it out. It really was heavy.

She searched it hastily, heart pounding at every noise

from the corridor. If she heard them coming, she could shove the case back in place and make up an excuse for being there, but she had to be quick if she was going to find anything. And no Le Goffian half measures. She felt in every pocket, shook out every shoe, and peered at hairbrushes and hats for any unexpected bumps. She double-checked that all the pear drops really were pear drops. She unstopped a bottle of perfume that smelled overwhelmingly of Ester – a sugary sort of rose – and examined the elaborate stopper, looking for the red wink of a diamond. Nothing.

And at that moment the train gave a huge jolt, and a bag fell from the rack overhead, smashing into the bottle.

Glass shards rained on to the floor. Perfume sloshed all over Max, who instantly smelled of a whole *garden* of roses. A lot went on the spider as well, who waved his legs at her in reproach. In the world of spiders, rose perfume is very much *not-flies*.

But there was no time to worry about the spider, because just then Max heard someone coming up the corridor, with the footsteps of a man built like a small mountain. A man recruited by Die Eiserne Hand. A man who could very easily throw you off a train if he found you meddling where you shouldn't meddle.

She shoved the suitcase back in place, but there was still the small matter of the glass all over the floor, and the shards that were clinging to her jumper, and the fact that she smelled like a hundred Esters all at once. The stopper of the bottle rolled pointedly across the floor. (It hit the spider, which was definitely not-flies; and it is a shame that spiders don't understand the idea of bad luck, because this spider was certainly having some.)

From what Max could make out, Klaus had paused to coo at the crying baby that she had heard earlier. She had to think fast.

Above her there was a window showing a slice of sky, set into a square of metal in the ceiling. It looked a bit like her own skylight, except that under the window were the words *SADECE ACIL DURUMLAR*. Max didn't speak Turkish, but the words were in the shade of red that always means *emergency* and *danger*, wherever you go.

Well, this *was* an emergency. And small slices of sky,

you will remember, made Max feel like she could go anywhere and do anything.

Sometimes, this feeling was a bit misleading. Other times, like now, it was very stupid.

When Klaus's footsteps resumed, Max was already on the seat, and undoing the catch on the emergency roof hatch. Half a second later, she was scrambling up on to the back of the seat, and poking out through the roof.

The little slice of sky opened out into huge-huge-endless sky, and howling wind, and suddenly Max was a lot less sure about her plan; but by this time she looked as suspicious as it was possible to look, and Klaus would *certainly* know what she had been up to. And she *really* didn't want to be thrown off a train in the middle of the Bulgarian countryside. So she wriggled her legs through, crouched on the roof of the train, and slammed the hatch shut.

She was just in time. But there was no time for relief: there was only horror.

Wind screamed past her as though it was fleeing something, and it pulled at her skin as if it would tear it from the bones, and battered her lungs when she tried to breathe. The rain flew at her. The noise deafened her. She had to get back inside.

She began to crawl, very slowly, plaits flying behind her like flags.

She only just saw the tunnel in time.

Throwing herself flat on the train, Max barely missed the tunnel roof. The frozen air of the tunnel hit her like a wall of water. For a few long seconds, there was only blackness, and the tortured wind. Then they burst back out again.

She crouched, now alert for anything overhead, and when she felt sure of her balance she began to crawl up to the end of the carriage. The gap between this carriage and the next turned her stomach. But there was no other way forward, and Max had to find the next door. She stretched forward her hands first – then followed them with her right foot, then her left – and crossed the divide.

She carried on crawling. This must be, she thought, what the spider felt like. Scuttling along in a world that was enormous and full of meaningless noise and always

likely, with a sudden swoop, to kill you.

Being a spider, she decided, was horrendous.

At last, she reached the next hatch. She had to lie flat for a minute more to avoid some low-hanging wires that crackled and sparked as the train passed. Then she heaved the hatch open, wriggled her body around (oh, horrible, horrible) – and clambered, shaking, back into the train.

She was at the end of a corridor. It was empty. She collapsed with relief on to the floor.

*It was stupidly dangerous*, said Sister Marguerite's voice in her head. *But since you've pulled it off, I'm glad.*

For several minutes, Max just lay there in the blissful quiet, curled up tight, shaking. All her resolve began to weaken. She missed Sister Marguerite and her mother and her home and she wanted, more than anything, to just be taken care of for a moment. But nobody was going to do that.

Then she had a thought, and the thought was enough to make her get up and clean her blackened hands, even though they still shook; and go to her carriage for clean clothes that wouldn't give her away with the stink of roses; and hasten back one more time to the carriage of Klaus Grob and Ester Rosenkrantz, before Ester recovered from the spider.

This was the thought:

She had never noticed that there was more than one way into a train before. It had never occurred to her to look. Would she have noticed if there was more than one way into a suitcase? And that suitcase had been *much* heavier than it should have been.

Celeste was *still* in the corridor – as always – and there was no way for Max to avoid her gaze. She watched Max hurry back and forth, eyebrows raised. "Busy day, Max?" she asked.

But Celeste was a lot less scary now that Max had spent time clinging to the roof of a train. So she just said "Yep!" and charged past, leaving Celeste to stare after her, and wonder.

Ester and Klaus were still gone: the spider had done well. Everything but Ester's pear drops was in exactly the same position. Klaus must have just reached in and grabbed them, not spotting the glass. Max pulled the suitcase out again.

She heaved it on to each side in turn, searching.

There! A long, thin hole, hidden on the bottom edge. A hole that just might take a key.

Ester and Klaus had left their coats behind. Max searched the pockets. Klaus's were no use, and Ester's had a lot of sticky pear drops. Max was so close, but still so infuriatingly far. She tried putting her chin on her hands to channel Sister Marguerite, and she *thought*.

If she had a key like that, she would want to keep it with her at all times. Not just in a coat or a skirt or anything, that you had to take on and off. It might, she thought glumly, be with Ester right now. Probably on a chain round her neck – although, no, Max would have seen it nestled among her fabulous necklaces.

There was a click-clicking noise from the corridor, and Max tensed – but it was just a grumble from the train, not a tapping stick. The stick was still here, anyway, Max remembered. Ester must really have been scared, to race off without it; she *always* had that stick with her.

And then, half a second later, the penny dropped.

Max grabbed the stick and twisted at the silver top. Like a dream, it turned, then eased away from the wood. Peeking out from the bottom of the silver was something long, thin, and gold, with little ridges along the edge. Max slid it out of its hiding hole. A tiny key.

Heart hammering, Max put the key in the lock, turned it, and opened the *other half* of Ester Rosenkrantz's suitcase. It was stuffed full of jewels.

Rubies and sapphires and diamonds. Emeralds and opals. Jade and topaz and musgravite. Amber and onyx. They glittered under the train's electric lights. They winked and shimmered. They were blindingly beautiful.

And that is why Max didn't see Ester and Klaus standing in the doorway, until Ester began to bellow at the top of her appalling lungs.

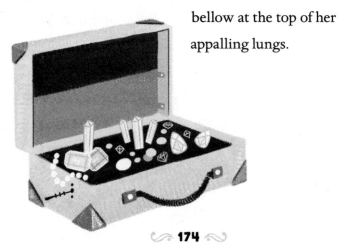

# 10

## ISTANBUL AT DAWN

The bellowing brought the train guard, a man with a face as heavy and folded as a bulldog's, who shook all his folds in outrage at Max. Max spoke neither Romanian nor Turkish, so she couldn't explain that the jewels she appeared to be stealing were, in all likelihood, stolen goods already. Even if she *could* explain, she was not sure that this particular guard would take any notice. The head shaking was keeping him very busy, and he seemed to be enjoying himself.

Max tried to scrabble through the jewels and find the tiny heartbreak diamond, but that only resulted in a lot more yelling, and the guard pulling her off the case and down the corridor.

So that is how she ended up locked in the guard's carriage, while the guard phoned somebody about her, glaring at her and wobbling his face about in disgust.

The guard's carriage was dingy and uncomfortable, and it was hard being told off so unfairly, but as Max's heart finally started to slow down it occurred to her that this might not be so bad. She was safe, here, from any pushing-off-train business. She had done it – she had found a secret stash of jewels, smuggled in a hidden compartment and guarded by a member of the shadowy Die Eiserne Hand, and if that didn't turn out to hold the heartbreak diamond she would eat her own knitted bobble hat. They would have to find someone who could speak French eventually, and if she was being handed in as a thief, then she would meet exactly the right people to arrest Ester and Klaus and find Marguerite. When they looked in that case, which the guard had insisted on keeping safe in his room, then they would know that she was telling the truth. She just had to wait.

So her tired brain gave in for the day, and she settled into the hard chair that she had been given, leaned against the window, and shut her eyes.

It was a long, long night. The guard played games of backgammon with himself most of the time, and he kept shaking his head sadly and sighing, so presumably he was losing. The pale electric light was kept on, and the seat was uncomfortable. Max could only doze in fits. Sometimes she wasn't sure if she was awake or dreaming. Was Klaus really at the door, looking wide-eyed and worried at her? Was Celeste really there, shouting furiously at the guard? Was her mother really there, telling her not to ruin her appetite for dinner?

Questions wandered sleepily around her brain, although she was no longer trying to answer them. What were all the other jewels in that suitcase? Was Celeste Celeste, or was she Suzanne – and why had she followed Ester and Klaus? And then there was Rupert – why had he been pushed, and what was the secret behind his phone call, and his strangely empty bag? Ester must be the thief, Max was sure of it, but there were still a lot of things that she didn't understand.

If she *had* understood those things, she might not have been quite so relieved when dawn began to break, and brought with it a shadowy skyline of domes and tower blocks and minarets, and the Bosfor delivered her at last to her final destination:

*Istanbul.*

The sky was a pale yellow, and hung with mist. Max watched it brighten in peace. It was beautiful. Then the station came into sight, and the fuss began.

The train guard had moved on from shaking his head, and now started jerking it instead, to show Max that she was to get up and follow him. Max tried the word "breakfast", but it got no response. So she sighed, wound her scarves round herself tightly, and followed.

The guard hurried her along at high speed. She craned around as they left, but didn't see Ester, Klaus, or Celeste-or-Suzanne – it would have been comforting, somehow, to see a face she knew. She missed Marguerite, and she even missed the silly smile of Rupert Nobes.

She had no time to take in Sirkeci station. All she had was an impression of pink and white, and beautiful round glass windows; and then she was being taken through a small door, and up and down stairs, and the noise of the crowds got fainter and fainter.

The guard opened a door, which led to a small dim room. He shook his bulldog folds in greeting at the figure inside, glared at Max once more for luck, and plodded away again to get on with glaring at his next passengers.

The figure in the room nodded at Max, like an egg wobbling on a spoon. Max was finally looking at a familiar face.

"Commandant Le Goff!"

"Good morning. Maximilienne, isn't it? We received a call as soon as the guard found it in the luggage. I was flown over at once." He said this in an aggrieved tone, as if it was all rather tiresome and unfair.

It made Max feel a bit giddy to think that all those miles, all those Hungarian fields and Romanian forests and Bulgarian valleys, could be skipped over in a few hours on an aeroplane. All she could think of to say was "Hello", which seemed to fall a bit short.

"*So,*" Le Goff said, with a saintly effort to take an interest, "we finally found a Phantom."

Max could have cried with relief. "Yes!" she said, beaming.

"I wouldn't look so pleased, Max," said Le Goff, with a sigh. "It's extremely serious. Take a seat, please."

Max thought that this was rather joyless of him, but she sat down and worked at straightening her face. Then she remembered the questions she had to ask, and she didn't have to work at it any more. "Do you know they got Sister Marguerite?" she asked. "Are you looking for her?"

Commandant Le Goff had a go at looking like a man who knows what's going on, for about three seconds. Then he scratched his head, and said, "Do I know that who got who?"

"Ester and Klaus! They got my friend. The nun. She didn't get on to the Bosfor."

"Ah, yes. Your accomplice," said Le Goff. "I was wondering where she'd got to. Yes, we'll certainly be looking for *her*."

Accomplice?

"Hang on," said Max, "who do you think stole the diamond?"

"We were hoping," replied Le Goff, "that *you* would tell *us*."

"Ester Rosenkrantz!"

Commandant Le Goff frowned. "Don't be *difficult*,

Max." He had the pained face of a man who had already dealt with Ester Rosenkrantz, and had absolutely no interest in dealing with her again unless it was entirely necessary. "Come on now. You're only a child. You'll be in much less trouble if you tell us what you know."

"But why am I in trouble?"

At last Commandant Le Goff understood that they were not on the same page. He sighed.

"Look, Max, we know you were the smuggler. The guard searched your things last night." He gestured to a table in the corner of the room. "And I am asking you, *nicely*, who you were working with. But you are testing my patience."

Max looked at the table. Her brown case was there, opened up, and next to it was the bobble hat from Great-Aunt Elodie. Except that it wasn't a bobble hat any more – the bobble had been unravelled, leaving a surprisingly small heap of wool. And on top of that heap sat a sparkling red stone, not more than two inches wide, with a white streak across the middle.

"Not the wimple," said Le Goff, "but the

bobble hat. You two and your stupid sense of humour! Well, the joke's over, Maximilienne."

"There's been some mistake," said Max, hardly able to take it in. "That hat is from my great aunt. I have her letter to prove it."

. . . except, she realized, that she didn't. Her letter was at 21 Téli Út with Istvan Marek. Or, more likely, in a bin somewhere in Hungary.

How had the diamond got into her hat? Or – had it been there all along? Max remembered the newspaper article: *it is not known when the real diamond was removed.* Somebody could have slipped it in before she even left – before she even got the parcel.

"My great-aunt," she repeated faintly. "You should ask her. Elodie Morel. She can tell you. It was just a hat."

Le Goff just raised an eyebrow about half a

centimetre, before realizing that was tiring and putting it back down again. "Madame Morel is on her way," he said. "We phoned the number on your luggage label and explained the situation. In the meantime, Max, I suggest you give some thought to *cooperating.*"

There was a long silence, as Max tried to make sense of what was happening. The first early cars grumbled below. The room was icily cold, and Max was hungry: it was difficult to think straight.

"But what about Ester's case?" she managed at last. "All those jewels? And Klaus? He was there as security. . ."

Le Goff had started wearily filling out a form, and didn't look up, but recited flatly: "Madame Rosenkrantz took the decision to remove her jewels from Fort Vaults after the incident with the masked robbers, the week before the Phantom theft was discovered. She was, I believe, hoping to sell a few, and deposit the others with a security firm in Turkey, who are currently thought to be the best in the world. Naturally, she was concerned for their security; but she didn't want to draw attention to their presence by sending them under official protection. So she brought them herself, with the security fellow *incognito.*"

It had been there in the article, Max remembered: *many are taking steps to move their most valuable jewels to new secret locations.* And she had *known* that Ester stored her jewels at Fort; Marguerite had said so. She had been so close – she was right that Klaus was security, and right that Ester was hiding diamonds – but she had imagined all the wrong reasons. No wonder Ester had been so angry when Klaus had left the suitcase unguarded in the lockers, back at the Budapest baths.

There was a knock on the door, so gentle it was almost a scrabble. They both looked towards the scrabble-knock, unsure if it had really been a knock at all, or just a noisy bit of air. Then a voice like tiny bells said, "Commandant?" – and air doesn't do *that.* So Commandant Le Goff opened the door.

The woman who swept in was covered in lace and jewels. Her small, pointy face was set in a permanent half smile, and her bright little eyes darted constantly about the room. She wore a lot of rouge, and reminded Max forcefully of the pink sugar mice that were always in the window of a sweet shop near her school.

"Maximilienne! My, how like your *maman* you are!" she trilled, ignoring Le Goff entirely. "Now, what *is* going on, my dear? These silly policemen seem to think you have a *diamond*." And she laughed – like glasses chinking, like icicles falling, like pixies crying.

"I don't know what happened," said Max. "It was in the hat you sent me."

Le Goff, his egg-face full of huff over the "silly policemen" comment, indicated the table. "You are familiar with this bobble hat, madame?"

Great-Aunt Elodie looked at the hat. She darted her eyes to Max, Le Goff, the hat again, the window, Le Goff, Max, the hat – all in a speedy second – and blinked innocently.

"No," she said.

Max found, to her surprise, that she was standing. "That is not TRUE!" she yelled. "*You* sent me that hat. And Marguerite is missing, Commandant, and somebody has to help. And Rupert was pushed off a train, and Celeste is actually called Suzanne, and..." *Come on*, Max scolded herself. *Make sense.*

"Commandant," said Great-Aunt Elodie. She placed a

gloved paw on Le Goff's arm. "My great-niece is obviously distressed. May I have some time alone with her?"

She had a way of asking a question that wasn't really asking. Le Goff was nodding before she had even finished the sentence. "Of course," he said. "I'll go and inform Madame Rosenkrantz of developments here. I'll have to lock the door, I'm afraid." He started towards the door, remembered something, and turned back to pocket the diamond and take it with him. Great-Aunt Elodie's eyes followed every movement.

The door shut with a heavy bang.

Max's great-aunt settled herself on the chair and looked up at Max. She made her voice even tinier and softer, so that it wouldn't carry through the door.

"We set everything up perfectly," she said. "You had one simple little thing to do, my dear. How precisely did you make such a mess of it?"

Max felt a bit winded. Somehow she had not quite believed, until her great-aunt spoke, that the sugary old lady had done this on purpose. She had been willing it to be some terrible mistake. But now that Great-Aunt Elodie had dropped the small smile, and clenched her gloved paws in her lap, Max suddenly found it all too easy to believe.

"So this *was* all you! *You're* behind the Phantoms?" Max didn't think she had ever loathed anybody this much. "Where's Marguerite?"

For the benefit of Le Goff's retreating ears, Great-Aunt Elodie said loudly, "I don't know what you're talking about, my dear. *Do* calm down." Then her voice dropped back to its silky murmur – like shadows humming, like snails sharing secrets. "I have no idea, my dear, and I don't care. Suzanne took care of her, I presume. She is very efficient at handling people who get in the way."

Suzanne! So she was in league with Max's great-aunt! It must have been her, then, who had been "efficient" with Rupert, when he wouldn't leave her alone. Max struggled to hold everything straight in her head. "So she *is* Suzanne?" she said. "Not Celeste Le Blanc?"

Great-Aunt Elodie's eyes fixed on Max for a full half-second before darting off again. "I don't know why you know that name, Maximilienne. You seem to be a *meddler*. I wrote letters to Celeste Le Blanc, but she doesn't exist. The letters were addressed to an abandoned house. That way, even if anyone suspected that Suzanne was one of us, they still wouldn't find our letters. I prefer letters to phone calls after the fiasco with the tiara, but we still have to be very careful."

"Then how did Suzanne get..." Max began – and then she suddenly remembered Klaus's voice: *Suzanne Leroy, works at the post office...* Of course! If Suzanne worked at the post office, then she didn't need to wait for the letters to arrive. She had been able to take them before they were even delivered.

Great-Aunt Elodie ignored the half question. She seemed to be speaking to herself now, as much as Max. "Celeste is quite a new creation. We had to switch addresses and names when we found our old route was being tampered with," she said, pouting, as if this had been very unfair. "I suppose that was your precious Marguerite. Anyway, after we discovered that, we could hardly risk Suzanne smuggling the diamond herself. Even if she changed trains, the snoop might follow her – we didn't know how much they knew about us. We needed to change our plan invisibly, so that they wouldn't even realize we had changed it."

"Ideally, we needed a new smuggler – someone totally unconnected, and totally above suspicion. Which is difficult, my dear." She sighed sweetly at the unfairness of her life. "So, I tried calling your parents. I knew they would never deign to come themselves, but if they sent one of the children, that would be perfect. Nobody would never expect a child."

"I wasn't very hopeful, my dear, knowing your family. I was up all night dreaming up other schemes. But then they sent you – the *youngest*! The perfect smuggler. So I sent a hat, and all Suzanne had to do was open it up at the post office, add the bobble and send it on its way.

"It was all set up perfectly," she said. Her little hands clenched in their gloves with frustration. "Suzanne's theft went flawlessly, she slipped it in the bobble without any trouble, and I reminded your dear mother to make *absolutely* sure you packed the hat. All you had to do was get from A to B, while Suzanne kept an eye out. I didn't think you'd be a *meddler*. None of the rest of your family are."

"The photograph," said Max, "That you sent to Cel –
to Suzanne. It was of me, wasn't it?"

Great-Aunt Elodie inclined her head once: yes. "One
of the photos that your dear mother so thoughtfully
sends me every Christmas."

"M. For Elodie *Morel*," murmured Max, talking to
herself now. *Take great care, my dear! Never has a girl been
more precious.* The girl in the letter wasn't Suzanne. It
was her, Max.

No wonder Suzanne had seemed so angry when Max
had nearly left her case behind on the Kálmán Imre. All
that time she spent standing around in train corridors,
she had been keeping watch on Max's car. And she
hadn't been following Ester and Klaus at all, that day in
Budapest – she had been following *Max*. Following the
heartbreak diamond.

Great-Aunt Elodie Morel and Max Morel both sat
silently, both with brains whirring, both trying to plan
their next steps – more alike than Max knew or would
want to admit. The room was very still and quiet.
Nothing rattled or chugged or swayed. Max wished
she was still on a train somewhere, speeding off into

possibilities: she seemed to have hit a dead end.

She remembered the park in Budapest, where she had felt as though all of them were tangled together, in ways that she couldn't quite unravel. Now she saw how the tangle had happened: Marguerite was chasing a diamond, Ester and Klaus were protecting their diamonds, Suzanne was guarding a diamond – and Max *had* a diamond, all along.

She would bet good money that Rupert Nobes had not been with them by coincidence, but she couldn't see yet how he fit in to it all. She wondered if she would ever know. Poor Rupert, still lying in hospital somewhere back in Romania. And Sister Marguerite – where was she now?

The silence was broken by Le Goff, knocking smartly on the door before letting himself in.

"You have another visitor, Max," he said. "She has just arrived. But we'll be arresting her as well."

Max's heart leaped. That could only mean one thing.

"Sister Marguerite?"

# 11

## A CUPBOARD IN SIRKECI STATION

And it really was.

Le Goff nodded a small, tired nod. "I'll bring her now. Madame Morel, there is some paperwork to discuss with you, as Max's acting guardian. . ."

"Of course. I will say goodbye to my great-niece," tinkled Great-Aunt Elodie, "while you fetch the nun." It was not a question. Le Goff nodded, and left.

Max put her face in her hands and took several steadying breaths. Until now, she had not really let herself think her fears out loud. But Marguerite was alive. It was all right. *It was all right.*

When she raised her head, Great-Aunt Elodie was standing by the table with the contents of Max's case and the empty bobble hat. Max was sure she saw her gloved paw twitch something quickly out of sight.

"What are—" she began – but then Le Goff arrived,

and she could hear Marguerite's singsong voice nattering behind him, and she forgot to finish the question. Le Goff signalled for Marguerite to wait and *be quiet*, as he took his leave of Great-Aunt Elodie, who apologized *very* sadly for Max.

"She is just a child, officer," she sighed. "It seems this nun must be the real menace."

"Quite so, madame."

"Could I see it?" she asked, with a small porcelain smile. "The little diamond causing all the trouble? If it's not too rude to ask; I realize you are doing a *very* stressful job here, Commandant. . ."

Le Goff was obviously pleased that somebody finally appreciated this. He coughed importantly, and held up the diamond for her to inspect. She ran a gloved finger over it in wonder.

And then a flurry of things happened very fast:

Le Goff returned the diamond safely to his pocket, and said goodbye to Great-Aunt Elodie. She sailed from the room.

Sister Marguerite flew in wimple first, tripping over something. She grabbed at Le Goff for balance, who peeled her off with distaste.

From somewhere outside, Ester started bellowing. Le Goff sighed and left the room, locking the door behind him.

That was all: nothing that seemed important. All this happened in seconds – in the blink of a beady, bright little eye – as fast as the flutter of a phantom.

Marguerite ran to Max and enveloped her in a huge habit-hug. Max hugged tightly back, and despite all the steady breathing, she found that she was crying in extremely squiggly breaths now, gasping in and out.

Marguerite squeezed tightly. "I'm sorry I'm late, *mon lapin!*"

For a few moments, they just hugged, not speaking. Outside, Istanbul was waking. The sound of traffic was by now a steady thrum, and sometimes you could make out a raised voice – presumably speaking Turkish, but it was too far away for Max to hear any words.

"I came as soon as I could," said Marguerite. "I got the first flight out of Bucharest."

"I thought you were – that someone might have—"

"Well, I'm not and they didn't," said Marguerite,